Miguel eyed the bat still clutched in Jennifer's hand.

He spread his arms, palms up, and stated the obvious. "I'm not dead."

She dropped the bat. It bounced once before toppling over. Then she breathed his name. "Miguel."

In those two syllables, she expressed all the hope, longing and love that had kept him alive for a year and a half in captivity.

He closed the space between them and swept her into his arms, holding her body so close he couldn't tell where his ended and hers began. He pressed his lips against her soft hair, the blond strands almost glowing in the dark as if they had collected all of the moonlight.

She wrapped her arms around his waist, tilting her head back, her cheeks wet. "My every prayer has been answered, but how... Why did they tell me you were dead?"

The navy and the CIA had their reasons, but he didn't need to tell her those reasons—right now.

POINT BLANK SEAL

CAROL ERICSON

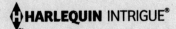

For my two Wildcats

Recycling programs
for this product may
not exist in your area.

ISBN-13: 978-0-373-75705-3

Point Blank SEAL

Printed in U.S.A.

www.Harlequin.com

Carol Ericson is a bestselling, award-winning author of more than forty books. She has an eerie fascination for true-crime stories, a love of film noir and a weakness for reality TV, all of which fuel her imagination to create her own tales of murder, mayhem and mystery. To find out more about Carol and her current projects, please visit her website at www.carolericson.com, "where romance flirts with danger."

Visit the Author Profile page at Harlequin.com.

CAST OF CHARACTERS

Jennifer Lynch—When her fiancé and the love of her life is presumed dead, Jennifer carries on for the child who will never meet his father, but when her fiancé shows up on her doorstep very much alive but psychologically wounded, Jennifer must fight to bring him back from the brink.

Miguel Estrada—This navy SEAL sniper was captured and tortured, only the love for his fiancée keeping him strong, so when he escapes he returns to his fiancée a broken man but determined to keep his family safe from the dark forces closing in on him.

Mikey Estrada—The son born while Miguel was in captivity; now Miguel will do whatever it takes to keep his son safe, even if that means staying away.

Rob Eastwood—Miguel's brother is a "fixer" for Hollywood, but can he fix what's wrong with Miguel?

Maggie Procter—A nurse at the rehab facility where Miguel went for recovery pretended to be his friend when he was there, but her mysterious actions indicate she may be working with the enemy.

Angela Woodruff—The director of the rehab center may only be following orders, but those orders could lead to Miguel's capture and torture.

Vlad—A sniper for the insurgents during the Gulf War has begun assembling an international terrorist network and has contacts within the US intelligence community willing to do his bidding—including neutralizing Miguel Estrada.

Ariel—The mysterious head of the Vlad task force, Ariel is willing to reveal herself to help Miguel catch a traitor.

Prologue

A light glimmered among the rocks to his right, and Miguel Estrada shifted his MK 15 in response, his heart thudding against his chest. He whispered into the mic clipped to his flak jacket. "Twenty degrees to your right, up another thirty yards."

Miguel couldn't tell if the SEALs on the ground were following his directions or not. They'd moved out of his view behind some rocks, and they couldn't answer him and risk giving away their position. He just had to trust they'd heard him and reacted accordingly, especially since this wasn't his regular team and they were missing that natural rapport.

His world became the area in his scope, and his eyeball tracked back and forth to scan that world, looking for any movement or more light.

These caves tucked into the rugged interior of Afghanistan were a maze, deep and complex.

The intelligence they'd received on the where-abouts of Vlad had led a team of SEALs, including him on sniper duty, to this godforsaken part of the world.

The intel suggested Vlad would be lightly guarded and relaxed, not suspecting the hell about to be unleashed upon him. Miguel just hoped Vlad didn't have any children with him. That made everything more complicated—like the two boys the team had run into on their trek up here.

Thank God, it hadn't been Miguel's call to make on how to deal with the boys. Elias had decided to release them, and it looked like that had been a good call since they hadn't seen them—or anyone else—since those boys had scampered across the rocks.

A light flickered again in the same area, and Miguel held his breath, waiting for an opportunity. If he could take out Vlad or anyone with Vlad from this vantage point, he'd do it and save the SEALs clambering over those boulders a few bullets.

The night scope on his sniper rifle cast a green glow on the rugged terrain, with every rock and every edge standing out in stark relief. If only he could see a person, other than the SEALs, he could help verify this location for them.

The brush behind him rustled and he tensed his muscles. He could probably handle one of those little gerbils or moles, but if that was a bat flapping his wings behind him he just might lose it.

Miguel tapped his fingernail against the trigger. Snipers generally had all the patience in the world, but those SEALs down there should've emerged from that cluster of boulders by now. Maybe they'd discovered something out of his sight. Miguel's own team would've found a way to signal that news.

He licked the grit from his lips and shifted his rifle again, zeroing in on the area where the SEALs had disappeared earlier. If they'd gotten his message, they should've popped up twenty degrees to the right of the jagged outcropping that looked like a mouthful of bad teeth.

He mumbled under his breath, "C'mon, guys."

A shift and a scrape behind his location had the hair on the back of his neck quivering. Before he had time to analyze this latest noise behind him, movement on the rocks below had him tightening his finger on the trigger. A light flashed behind the rocks and a pop echoed in the distance.

What the hell just happened? Miguel hissed into his mic, "What was that? Send me a signal."

The only signal he received was another flash and bang. Had the SEALs come upon Vlad's hideout? Were they taking him out now?

The crack of a twig behind him didn't sound

like a nighttime rodent or even a bat, but his mission right now was to protect those men down there. Breathing heavily, Miguel swept the rocky hillside, looking for anything that hadn't been there before.

He hadn't liked the look of those particular rocks from the get-go, but the team had to traverse them to get to Vlad's cave—if that *was* Vlad's cave.

A head rose above the highest boulder and Miguel's gut lurched. A man, a keffiyeh wrapped about his head, waved his arms in the air, a weapon clutched in one hand.

Miguel swallowed hard as he recognized the weapon. Then he swore when he realized the man was gesturing—toward him…or someone behind him.

In a split second, he took the shot and dropped the man while he was still waving. Then he rolled to his side, hauling his rifle with him, but it was too late. As he tried to reposition his weapon to the target behind him, he heard the click of a gun.

A heavy boot crushed his arm holding the rifle and Miguel gritted his teeth. Someone else kicked him in the head, and the tinny taste of blood flooded his mouth.

A man growled in English, "Drop your weapon and get on your knees. Your team members are all dead."

Instead of releasing his rifle, Miguel swung it behind him, making contact with someone's leg. The target grunted and one of his cohorts kicked Miguel in the midsection.

The cold metal of a gun pressed against Miguel's temple.

"I'm going to tell you one more time. Release your weapon and get on your knees."

They seemed to have given up on the idea of Miguel releasing anything because someone began to pry his fingers off the rifle, bending them back and breaking a few in the process. They weren't about to wait for him to get on his knees either, as he was yanked up by his jacket.

Miguel raised his eyes for the first look at his captors. Three men—one pointing a gun at his head, one rubbing his shin and the third assessing him through narrowed eyes.

Miguel cleared his throat and spit some blood out of the side of his mouth. "Was this a trap?"

His question earned him another kick to the gut, and he doubled over.

There was no way anyone could've known their position, even if those two boys from earlier in the day had ratted them out, which they probably had. This had been a setup from the start, and in the off chance that he got out of this alive, he'd make it his life's mission to root out the mole that had been responsible for the deaths of those SEALs down there.

"We ask the questions, pig. How much do you know about the man you call Vlad?"

Since Miguel had no intention of answering any of their questions—now or ever—it looked like he wouldn't get that chance to track down the mole.

He spit blood again, this time at his interrogator's foot. "Go to hell."

As the butt of his own rifle came at his head, Miguel had one thought before the darkness engulfed him.

Jennifer.

Chapter One

Two years later

Jennifer herded her fifth-grade students into the park and yelled at two boys straggling behind. "Chase and Noah, you are not in middle school yet. I can still keep you from walking at promotion this week."

The two boys laughed and shoved at each other, but they caught up with the class.

Jennifer pressed the smile from her lips. She couldn't help it if she had a soft spot for rambunctious boys. Her own son kept her on her toes and he was only eighteen months old.

When her class got to the picnic area with the other fifth-grade classes already there, she set them free and she joined the other teachers by the barbecue area, sipping sodas and drinking from water bottles.

Jennifer pointed to the parents grilling the

burgers and hot dogs and setting out bags of chips. "Are we helping or what?"

Olivia Gutierrez, who had the classroom next to hers, shook her head and raised her can of soda. "Our wonderful parent volunteers are taking care of everything and told us to relax."

"We have the best parents." Jennifer stooped next to a cooler and pulled a bottle of water from the ice. She cracked open the lid and then tipped it toward a man at the edge of the parking lot next to the park. "Is that one of ours?"

Susan Burke, the other fifth-grade teacher at their school, shrugged. "I don't recognize him, but it's not like I've seen every parent in the fifth grade. Could be a parent from Stowe."

The man's attention seemed to float from the kids to the teachers, and a whisper of fear brushed the back of Jennifer's neck. She called to Mrs. Garrett, one of the teachers from Stowe. "Mrs. Garrett? Is that man in the blue shirt by the parking lot one of yours?"

Mrs. Garrett adjusted her glasses and squinted. "I've never seen him before, and I don't like the way he's looking at the kids."

Olivia smirked and elbowed Jennifer in the ribs.

"I'll find out right now." Mrs. Garrett, her gray, permed hair waving at the top of her head, marched toward the parking lot like an angry bird.

One of the other Stowe teachers laughed. "Once Pilar gets done with him, he's gonna wish he never set foot in this park."

Jennifer smiled, but her muscles tensed as she watched Mrs. Garrett confront the stranger.

Mrs. Garrett gestured toward the kids, waved her arms and pointed toward the barbecue area. When she was done with him, the man hightailed it back to his car.

Jennifer murmured, "Guess he wasn't a parent."

"What?" Olivia had turned around from her conversation with a parent.

Everyone else had lost interest in the confrontation. Nobody had watched Mrs. Garrett talk to the man…except Jennifer. She'd been very interested.

"The man at the edge of the parking lot. He left."

Olivia snorted. "Even if he'd been a parent, Mrs. Garrett had probably scared him off. She scares me."

Jennifer wiped her clammy palms on the thighs of her slacks and intercepted Mrs. Garrett when she returned to the barbecue area, her low heels clicking on the cement.

"Who was he?"

"Just an office worker from the area on his lunch break. He didn't realize the schools were having our end-of-the-school-year picnic today, but I set him straight."

Jennifer's gaze shifted to the squat office buildings scattered across the street from the park. If he worked in one of those, why had he driven a car and come through the parking lot? He should've crossed at the crosswalk and come in the way the kids had entered.

"Ms. Lynch, Ms. Lynch!" One of the girls from her class was waving her arms. "Do you want to do the Hula-Hoop with us?"

"Duty calls." She put her bottle of water on a picnic table and promptly forgot about the man in the parking lot as soon as she slipped that pink plastic circle around her waist.

After a few more games, a cheeseburger, a hot dog and enough candy to put her in a sugar coma, Jennifer clasped a clipboard to her chest and raised two fingers. "Anyone in my class leaving with a parent, check in with me before you take off."

Olivia bumped her shoulder. "With any luck, all of them will leave with a parent and we can stagger back to the school on our own."

"I doubt that's going to happen." Jennifer smiled at one of her free spirits, Chase, approaching with his mother. "Thanks for your help today, Mrs. Cannon."

"Thank you for a great school year and all

your understanding for our son. We're hoping Chase matures a little in middle school."

Jennifer's smile broadened. She hoped Mom wasn't counting too much on maturity in middle school, or she'd be heartily disappointed. "I'm sure Chase will do just fine in middle school. He won't have any problems with math. Right, Chase?"

"It's my favorite subject."

"I know it is."

For the next fifteen minutes, Jennifer continued to check out her students. Then she and the other fifth-grade teachers from Richmond gathered their classes, took a head count and started the trek back to the school.

When they reached the corner, Olivia shouted, "As soon as the light changes, cross the street, no dillydallying."

The kids, giggling at her word choice, surged into the street. Jennifer brought up the rear to make sure all the students made it into the crosswalk. As she glanced back toward the park, her heart stuttered when she spotted the so-called office worker Mrs. Garrett had set straight earlier.

Leaning against a car in the parking lot, he watched the students crossing the street. Or was he?

Jennifer couldn't tell the precise focus of his gaze from this distance, but he seemed to be looking at the back of the line…at her.

A horn beeped and she jumped. Everyone had made it across the street before the light changed, except her. She jogged to the curb as the kids laughed and called out, "C'mon, Ms. Lynch."

"Just showing what you're *not* supposed to do."

One of the girls, her face serious, grabbed Jennifer's hand. "You need to be careful, Ms. Lynch."

The girl's words caused a little trickle of fear to drip down her spine as her gaze darted to the park's now empty lot across the street.

"You're right, Maddy. I do."

LATER THAT EVENING, Jennifer cuddled her son, Mikey, against her chest, her feet kicked up on the coffee table. She pressed her face against his springy, dark hair and inhaled the scent of…toddler, very different from the scent of baby.

His lashes fluttered against his cheek, and she held her breath. She'd just gotten him to sleep after a wild play session that had involved cars, stuffed animals and crackers. She slid her feet from the coffee table and held Mikey close as she threaded her way through the toys on the floor to his bedroom. She liked that Mikey had his own room, even if they shared a bathroom. Two bedroom, one bath places in the nice areas of Austin weren't all that easy to find, but now she had to move.

She hadn't felt safe here ever since the break-in.

Kneeling next to Mikey's new toddler bed, shaped like a car, she pulled back the covers and tucked him in. She kissed his forehead and whispered, "Mommy loves you."

On the way out of the room, she flicked on his night-light. For being a fearless daredevil, Mikey didn't like the dark. She needed a night-light as much as he did these days.

After that day when she'd come home from picking up Mikey to find that someone had broken into her house, tossed it and had stolen some small electronics, she had a hard time falling asleep at night. Every little noise had her bolting upright in bed, and then lying awake the rest of the night with eyes wide-open.

She shuffled into the kitchen and uncorked a bottle of red. She splashed some into a glass and swirled it around before taking a sip. She took another sip and closed her eyes, allowing the warmth of the alcohol to seep into her tight muscles.

Having a drink shouldn't feel so good. She shouldn't let it feel so good—not with her mother's alcoholism running through her genes. Mom beat her drinking problem, but Jennifer would never let it get to that point. She sucked in another mouthful of wine and returned to the sofa, dragging a pillow into her lap.

Having Mikey had probably saved her from traveling down the same road as Mom. She couldn't be impaired and take care of her son. She'd never do that to him.

But, oh, those nights when Mikey stayed with Mom and Dad? The booze was the only thing that allowed Jennifer to forget.

A tear seeped from the corner of her eye. Who was she kidding? She'd never forget. Would never forget the day that crisp naval officer stood on her porch and delivered the news that would shatter her world.

She stabbed the power button on the remote and clicked through the channels, settling on a comedy she'd seen before. She couldn't laugh, not even with a half a glass of wine swirling in her veins.

As she switched the channel, the dog next door started barking. Max never barked unless something—or someone—wandered into his yard.

Jennifer set down the wineglass. On her way to the sliding door to the patio, she picked up a bat that she'd propped up in the corner of the room after the break-in. Staring outside, she flicked on the light, which illuminated the table, chairs and small barbecue that clustered on one side of the cement slab that passed for a patio.

The potted plants and flowers on the other side remained in darkness. She turned the light on and off again and then sucked in her lower lip.

The bulb on the left side of the door must've burned out. When had that happened? After the robbery, she'd checked all her locks and lights.

A dark shape moved in the shadows beyond the patio, and her knees almost buckled. Was that an animal? She cupped her hand at the glass and peered into the night.

She needed a dog. She needed a gun. She *had* a bat.

Hoisting the bat in one hand, she clicked the lock down and slid open the door. She advanced toward the dark side of the patio, raising the bat like Babe Ruth.

"Jennifer?"

She spun around and faced a man standing on her patio, bathed in an otherworldly light.

Her mouth dropped open and she grabbed on to a trellis rising from one of the pots.

"Jen, it's me. Miguel."

Miguel? It couldn't be. How much wine had she drunk in there? She cleared her throat and said the only thing that made sense. "You're dead."

Chapter Two

Miguel eyed the bat still clutched in Jennifer's hand. He didn't come this far to have it all end on her patio with a crushed skull, although he wouldn't blame her for taking a swing at him.

He spread his arms, palms up, and stated the obvious, "I'm not dead."

She dropped the bat. It bounced once before toppling over. Then she breathed his name. "Miguel."

In those two syllables, she expressed all the hope, longing and love that had kept him alive for a year and half in captivity.

She reached out her arms and seemed to sway toward him, her feet apparently rooted to the cement beneath them.

He closed the space between them and swept her into his arms, holding her body so close he couldn't tell where his ended and hers began. He pressed his lips against her soft hair, the blond strands almost glowing in the dark as if they had collected all of the moonlight.

She wrapped her arms around his waist, tilting her head back, her cheeks wet. "My every prayer has been answered, but how…? Why did they tell me you were dead?"

The navy and the CIA had their reasons, but he didn't need to tell her those reasons—right now.

"The navy thought I was dead. Everyone on that mission died."

She jerked in his arms. "Where have you been all this time?"

"I've been… I've been a prisoner of war." Was that a nice enough way to put it?

Gasping, she took his face in her hands. "Are you all right?"

"I am now." He kissed her lips and felt as if he were living a familiar dream, one that had kept him alive…and sane.

She returned his kiss like a woman starving. He broke away first as the passion rose, and she grabbed his hands.

"Come inside. You have to see Mikey. Miguel, we have a son."

He cupped her face with one hand, and smoothed the pad of his thumb across her cheek. "I know and I can't wait to see him, but I have to tread carefully."

"What are you talking about?" She tilted her head farther into his hand.

He touched his lips to her soft earlobe. "You had a break-in recently, didn't you?"

She drew back from him, her eyes wide. "How do you know that? How long have you been here, in Austin?"

"I'll tell you everything later, Jen." He jerked his thumb toward the small house where his son was sleeping. "There's something I need to do in the house first."

"What? Is Mikey in danger?"

"No." The lie felt right on his lips—for now. "Before we talk inside, I need to sweep the place for bugs."

If he discovered a hidden camera, that would be a different matter completely. He'd have to leave immediately.

"Why would someone want to bug my house?" She grabbed handfuls of his shirt and tugged.

"To get to me."

"I don't understand any of this, Miguel. I don't even know if you're really here."

"Oh, I'm here all right." He pressed another kiss against her lips to prove it.

"D-do I need to wait outside?"

"No, but when we're inside don't talk to me. Pretend you're alone."

"I can do that. I'm good at that."

He pinched her chin. "I'm sorry."

"Okay, let's do this. I'm getting cold." She rubbed her arms.

He stopped to pick up the bat and held it up. "Glad you still have my Louisville Slugger for protection."

"You almost got a hit upside the head for sneaking around out here." Pressing her fingers to her lips, she led him into the house and slid the door closed behind her.

Miguel's eye twitched as he watched Jennifer pluck up the wineglass from the coffee table and carry it into the kitchen. She'd vowed never to drink like her mother, but he guessed a dead fiancé and raising a child on your own could change plans.

He pulled the electronic bug detector from the front pocket of his jeans and began scanning the living room. He'd gotten lucky with the size of this house.

It shouldn't take him long to get through the house...and into the bedroom to see his son.

Jennifer rinsed her glass in the sink and turned toward him.

He put his finger to his lips and flicked the switch on his bug detector. He had it set to the display option. If there were any listening devices planted in Jennifer's house, he wouldn't want the sound of his bug sweeper to transmit to the people on the other end of the device.

Facing the wall, he waved the tracker from

corner to corner, sweeping across the bookshelf. The listening device would most likely be in this area, across from the TV.

Miguel's pulse jumped along with the squiggly red line on his tracker. He followed its lead and was rewarded with the gleam of a tiny mic wedged between two books.

He became aware of Jen hovering over his shoulder, and he jerked back. He pointed at the TV and then cupped his ear.

She dipped next to the coffee table and picked up the remote control. Aiming at the TV, she clicked, and the sound of a commercial jingle filled the small room.

Perfect. He plucked the listening device from its hiding place, and pinched it between his thumb and forefinger.

They'd hear a bunch of static on the other end and not much more. With the mic still squeezed between his two fingers, he mimed drinking a glass of water.

He didn't remember Jennifer being very good at charades but she was catching on quickly to this game.

She scurried in the kitchen and filled a glass with water from the tap. When she put it down on the kitchen table, he dropped the device in the water.

Her blue eyes widened as she stared at the black spec settling at the bottom of the water glass. She parted her lips, but he shook his head and placed two fingers against them.

This might not be the only bug in the place. He continued his search by sweeping the kitchen, but beyond a few false reads from the microwave, he found nothing there.

Swallowing hard, he moved toward the hallway. He turned into the first room on the right and turned on the bathroom light. He gestured toward the sink, and Jennifer cranked on the water.

His throat tightened when he saw the yellow rubber duck on the edge of the tub and the cartoon fish on the shower curtain. He'd missed so damn much.

A familiar sharp pain lanced the back of his head and he dragged in a long breath. He had to stay focused if he didn't want to miss even more of his son's life.

With the bathroom clear, Miguel turned back into the hallway, holding his breath. He stepped into his son's room, a gentle glow from a nightlight illuminating a path to his bed.

Miguel followed the light and crouched next to his son's bed. Pride and joy overwhelmed his senses, and he reached out and traced Mikey's chubby cheek with the tip of his finger. He wanted to gather the boy in his arms and never let go, but he had unfinished business.

Jen had come up behind him and squeezed his shoulder.

He covered her hand with his own and squeezed back, hoping to convey all his regret and sorrow at not being here with her during her pregnancy and the first year and a half of Mikey's life.

His nose stung, but he knew there would be no tears. He'd lost the ability to cry, but crouching here next to his son, inhaling the smell of his hair and skin, he knew he hadn't lost the ability to feel.

That thought had been the one thing that terrified him during his months of captivity.

Miguel pushed to his feet and scanned this room with even more vigor than the others. The guys who'd planted that bug obviously hadn't wanted to listen to the crying and fussing of a toddler.

Miguel shook his head at Jennifer and she straightened Mikey's covers before leading him out of the room.

When he walked into Jen's bedroom, the scent of her signature perfume hit him like a wave. Some nights he'd wake up in his cell smelling that fragrance. He knew it was a dream or hallucination at the time, but he'd wallowed in it anyway.

His gaze tripped over the king-size bed, and he momentarily squeezed his eyes shut. Had she shared that bed with anyone else since his…disappearance? He couldn't hold that against her if she did. She had every right to move on with her life.

But the way she'd kissed him and clung to him outside gave him a selfish hope that she hadn't.

He swept the room and got a hit. The blood boiled in his veins as he removed the device from a picture frame above her bed. He dropped that bug in the same glass of water and then finished his search of the rest of the house.

He tossed the bug detector on the kitchen counter and enfolded Jen in his arms again. "I'm just glad they didn't plant a camera, or all of that would've been for nothing."

She squirmed from his grasp and pressed her palms against his chest. "You're going to tell me what's going on, where you've been and why someone is bugging my house." Her fingers curled into the material of his shirt. "Not that I'm not thrilled you're back and safe, even if I am still pinching myself."

He took both of her hands and kissed one wrist and then the other. "Let's sit down."

"Do you want something to drink? To eat?" She skimmed her hands down his sides. "You've lost weight."

"I'll just get some water." He pushed aside the glass with the two bugs. "*Not* this glass."

She filled a glass with water from a dispenser in the fridge and handed it to him. "Let's talk."

As he followed her to the sofa in the living room, his mind whirled with images from the past two years of his life. What could he tell her? What would she want to hear?

The truth? Nobody could bear that. He'd barely survived it.

Jennifer sat on the sofa, curling one leg beneath her. "Can you start at the beginning?"

He settled beside her and draped an arm around her shoulders. "God, it's amazing to see you. Unbelievable."

"How do you think I feel? At least you knew I was alive. You even knew about Mikey…somehow." She threaded her fingers through his. "I thought— They told me you were dead."

"I'm sorry." He kissed the side of her head. "If I could take it all back, all those months, everything."

"The beginning, Miguel." She pursed her lips together in that schoolteacher way she had.

"We received some intel on Vlad. You remember I told you about him, right?"

"He was the sniper for the other side you guys kept coming up against until he disappeared from the field."

"He seemed to have dropped off the face of the Earth. We thought he might be dead, but we heard chatter and then received specific intelligence that he was regrouping in the caves of Afghanistan, which seemed totally likely."

"The last I heard from you was that you were going off on some assignment as a lone sniper, apart from your team."

"That assignment was tracking Vlad to his hideaway. I was pulled off a mission with my own team to help this one." He might be revealing classified information to Jen, but he didn't give a damn. The navy, his brothers, had never turned their backs on him, but he couldn't say the same for the shadowy intelligence agencies that called the shots.

"And it all went horribly wrong. The navy wouldn't tell me much, but I knew others had died with you." She bumped her knee against his. "Are they alive, too?"

"No. They're all dead."

She covered her eyes with one hand and sniffed. "So I'm the only one who gets the homecoming."

Miguel closed his eyes and clearly saw the ambush of the other SEALs at the cave, the pop of the guns, the flash of the gunpowder.

"What happened to you, Miguel?"

His lips twisted. "Do you have a few days?"

She snuggled closer to him and rested her head on his chest. "I have all the time you need, *mi amor.*"

Smiling, he ruffled her soft hair. He'd been

teaching her Spanish and she'd picked it up quickly, despite her atrocious accent.

"The mission went to hell. Someone set a trap. The SEAL team on the ground was ambushed and killed, and I was captured."

Her back rose and fell with quick, panting breaths. "H-how long? How long were you a prisoner?"

"Just over eighteen months."

She must've been doing the calculation in her head because her shoulders stiffened. She mumbled into his shirt. "Where have you been the past four to five months? Why didn't you contact me?"

"Various hospitals, starting with the one in Germany, debriefing sessions, intelligence meetings." He didn't mention the psychiatric units. He didn't want her pity.

She finally raised her head from his chest and met his gaze. "I'm sure you needed…treatment. I'm sure the navy and the CIA wanted to pick your brain. But those places didn't have telephones?"

"No. Literally, no. None for me anyway."

"They wouldn't allow you to use the phone?"

"No."

"And they wouldn't notify me? Your father? Your brother? Miguel, your father…"

"I know he's dead." His nostrils flared. "They

wanted you to go on believing I was dead, too. They still want you believing that."

Her eyes narrowed. "Those bugs you found—is that the navy, the FBI, some intelligence agency I don't need to know about?"

"It's not the navy. At least the navy is not calling the shots on this one."

"But you have reason to believe forces in the intelligence community broke into my home and planted listening devices?"

"Yes…maybe." He didn't know who was behind the sinister vibe he'd picked up at the debriefing center.

"Miguel, why? They should be treating you like the hero you are. They should be throwing you a ticker tape parade."

"Part of it is the sensitive nature of the assignment. They never went public with it."

"Part of it." She smoothed a hand across the shirt she'd wrinkled earlier. "What's the other part? Why wouldn't they allow you to contact me?"

Running a hand through his hair, longer than he usually wore it, he said, "I don't know."

"They don't know you're here."

"They don't know where I am, but I'm sure they can make an educated guess that I'm coming here."

"You spent eighteen months as a prisoner of war and now your own government wants to imprison you again?" Her cheeks flew red flags, indignation making her voice squeak.

"I don't know what they want, but I wasn't going to stick around anymore to find out." Guilt stabbed at his gut. The FBI had warned him that he could be putting Jennifer in danger by showing up on her doorstep, but he was afraid she already was in danger and he knew he was the only one who could protect her.

She trailed her fingertips along his tense jaw beneath his new beard. "What did your captors do to you, Miguel?"

"Tried to get information out of me." He rubbed a spot on his hip, still sore from the wounds he received from his captors.

"How?"

He thought he'd imagined the whispered question, spoken so softly, but the question lingered in Jen's blue eyes.

If he told her everything would it be worse than she imagined? He gazed into those baby blues and a knot tightened in his gut. Never.

"It was rough, Jen, but I'm here. I survived it." He brushed his lips across hers. "The thought of you gave me strength, pulled me through the most brutal moments of my captivity."

"How did you know I'd be waiting for you? You must've figured the navy would tell me you died. You didn't even know I was pregnant before you left. I didn't know I was pregnant."

"I tried not to think about it. Tried not to think of you moving on with someone else." He scooped her hair away from her face, his fingers tightening involuntarily. "Have you?"

"Of course not." Her lashes fluttering, she leaned in for the kiss he had waiting for her, and then she jerked back. "How did you know where I lived? How did you know about Mikey?"

"After the hospital in Germany, I went to a debriefing center near DC. I kept asking about you, kept asking for a phone. All they'd tell me was that you were okay and I needed to concentrate on getting better." He ground his back teeth. "As if seeing you wouldn't make me feel better immediately."

She grabbed his hands. "Did you escape this center? Leave without their permission?"

"Yeah, but not before breaking into an office and looking at my file." He pulled away from her and smacked a fist into his palm. "They didn't even tell me I had a son."

"A-are you AWOL or something?" Her gaze dropped to his clenched fist and then back to his face.

He shrugged, rolling his shoulders and flexing his fingers. "They debriefed me. It's not like I'm going to confess anything to you about my captivity or about Vlad that I didn't already spill to them."

"But you're not supposed to be here."

He ran a hand across his mouth. "This is the only place I'm supposed to be."

"I thought I was dreaming. I didn't think I'd ever see you again—except in those dreams."

He curled a hand around her neck and pulled her close, but before he could plant another kiss on her mouth, a crash resounded from the room next to them.

Then he smelled the smoke...and heard the screams of his son.

Chapter Three

Miguel bolted from the sofa and Jennifer lunged after him, tripping over the coffee table and banging her shin. The acrid smell of fire invaded her nostrils and terror ripped through her body like the jagged edge of a knife when she saw black smoke pouring out of Mikey's bedroom.

"It's Mikey's room."

Miguel charged into the smoke-filled room as Jennifer hung back coughing, her eyes watering. The heat from the flames licking at the drapes spiked her adrenaline, and she stumbled into the room after Miguel.

"Stay back, Jen. I've got him."

Miguel emerged from the dark gray cloud, Mikey clutched against his chest. He slammed the door behind him.

"Get out. Get out of the house now—back door."

She grabbed her phone on her way to the sliding glass door and gulped in the fresh air when she hit the patio. The smoke and fire from the front of the house hadn't made it back here yet, hadn't escaped from Mikey's room.

She got on the phone with 9-1-1 while stroking the back of Mikey's head as he sobbed against Miguel's shoulder. After giving emergency services the details, she held out her arms and Miguel transferred Mikey to her.

Even amid the terror, she couldn't help noticing how Mikey, in his fear, had clung to Miguel. She whispered in Mikey's ear, "It's okay. You're okay now. Mommy's here."

She rested her chin on top of Mikey's head and met Miguel's gaze as he pulled her away from the house. "What was that?"

"As far as I can tell from the smell, it was a Molotov cocktail."

"Meant for you? The FBI would go to those measures to get you back? Risk harming a child?"

Miguel cocked his head at the sound of sirens in the distance. "No, but who said I was being debriefed by the FBI?"

"You're scaring me even more, if that's possible." She squeezed Mikey so tightly, he squirmed in her grasp. At least the FBI had some accountability, rules to follow, public exposure. But these shadowy black ops organizations? Who held them accountable?

The sirens wailed louder, and Jennifer pointed to the side of the house. "Should we meet them?"

Her neighbor Stephen called over the back fence, "Is that you, Jennifer? What's going on?"

She yelled, "Fire in the front bedroom. Everyone's okay. I think the fire department just got here."

"Oh, my God. Mikey's room?"

"Yes, but he's fine. We're going out front now."

She led Miguel to the front of the house on the other side of where the fire was blazing.

Mikey lifted his head when they got to the street, now bathed in red light. Neighbors clustered on their porches in their pajamas. The firefighters started working before the trucks even came to a full stop.

Jennifer waved at a police officer getting out of his car, and he approached them.

"Is this your house, sir?"

Miguel pointed to her.

"I rent it. I live here with my son."

"Is the boy okay?"

"Scared but not injured." She shifted Mikey to her other hip.

"What happened?"

She felt Miguel stiffen beside her. They hadn't discussed what to tell the authorities. The truth?

"I—I'm not sure. We were talking in the living room, heard a crash from the front bedroom window and smelled smoke. I heard my son cry out, and my...friend went into the room and grabbed him. We all ran outside to the back of the house then, and I called 9-1-1."

"A crash, like a broken window?"

Miguel cleared his throat. "Like somebody threw something through the window."

The cop narrowed his eyes. "You know anyone who would do something like that, ma'am?"

"Of course not."

Taking out a notebook, the officer asked for their names.

Jennifer didn't blink an eye when she heard Miguel identify himself as Mike Esteban.

As they continued talking to the police officer, the firefighters seemed to be making short work of the fire that had engulfed Mikey's bedroom, where flames were shooting up to the roof through the broken window.

Mikey squirmed in her arms, kicking his legs against her hip.

"We need to stay here, Mikey."

"Do you want me to take him to watch? He seems interested, not scared."

Miguel hadn't even formally met Mikey yet. This was his first real contact with his son, and it couldn't be more disastrous.

With her throat tight, she spilled an all-too-willing Mikey into Miguel's outstretched arms and murmured, "He likes action. He's his father's son."

Miguel wandered to the other side of the house where Mikey could get a good look at the firefighters at work.

"Ms. Lynch, is that the boy's father?"

"N-no."

"Where's the boy's father?"

Was the officer trying to imply some former husband had a motive for firebombing her house? A case of jealousy while she enjoyed the company of another man?

"His father's dead."

"I'm sorry." He scratched his chin. "If what you heard is accurate, this sounds like a deliberate act. The arson investigators will do a full analysis, but I'm just trying to get as much information as I can from you to assist them."

"I understand. I'm a fifth-grade teacher at Richmond Elementary. I don't have any enemies that I know of and no irate parents that would go to these lengths."

"You never know what lengths people will go to—until they do."

Jennifer crossed her arms and shivered. "I suppose I'd better call the rental management company and let them know what happened."

The cop looked up from writing in his notebook, peering over her head at the house. "You won't be staying here tonight."

About an hour later, the fire chief on the scene

allowed her to go into the house to collect some of her things.

Miguel joined her inside the house, a sleeping Mikey nestled against his shoulder.

She touched Mikey's cheek. "Thanks for sitting in the car with him while I talked to the police and firefighters and called the rental agency. You even got him to sleep."

"After the excitement of watching the firefighters at work, he conked out." With one finger, Miguel pushed a lock of dark hair from Mikey's forehead. "He's incredible."

"You can put him on my bed while I pack up some of my stuff. The fire didn't get much farther than Mikey's room, but I'm going to have to replace his clothes. What the fire didn't destroy, the water did."

"It's just stuff." Miguel walked past her into the bedroom and put Mikey's head on the pillow.

A firefighter called into the house from the front door. "Folks, you're going to have to hurry it up."

"Just a few more minutes." She wheeled a suitcase from her closet and shoveled clothes into it. She dumped Mikey's dirty clothes from the laundry basket into a plastic bag and shoved that into the suitcase.

When she came out of the bathroom with a bag of toiletries, Miguel was on his knees by the side of the bed studying Mikey's face, stroking his hand with one finger.

Her nose tingled. Miguel's introduction to his son might not have been ideal, but Mikey had his father back and that's all that mattered.

"I'm ready. Did you come in a car?"

"It's a few blocks away." He slipped his arms beneath Mikey. "You can give me a ride to my rental and then follow me to my motel."

"I didn't even ask where you were staying."

"I think we had other things to talk about. The motel is here in Austin." Miguel put a finger to his lips, as they walked into the living room where the firefighter still hovered at the front door.

"Everything okay, folks?"

"Not perfect, but we're all safe." Jennifer grabbed her phone and laptop from the kitchen counter, and then shoved the computer into her school bag.

She still had to show up for class tomorrow and get through two more days of school.

With one arm still holding Mikey, Miguel took her bag from her and slung it over his shoulder.

When they got to her car, Miguel placed Mikey in his car seat and she buckled him in. "This takes some practice."

"I want to learn everything. I want to do everything, everything I missed."

She slammed the back door of the car and

kissed Miguel. "Thanks for getting Mikey out of that room."

"We got lucky. That was a small Molotov cocktail, never really exploded and didn't project far into the bedroom."

"We'll be in touch, ma'am."

She jerked her head to the side to acknowledge the firefighter. Had he heard Miguel? Did it matter? One of the firefighters had already mentioned something about a Molotov cocktail.

They weren't the suspects here.

She drove Miguel to his car a few blocks away and then followed him to his motel near the university.

He waved her into a parking spot in front of the two-story building while he swung into a space in a lot at the end of the building.

She waited in the car until he walked up to it. Then she released the trunk and he hauled out her suitcase and school bag.

She followed him to his room on the first level, carrying Mikey in her arms. She eyed the king-size bed and put Mikey in the middle of it.

The motel room had a little kitchenette and Jennifer wedged her back against the counter, folding her arms. "Now that we have some privacy, what do you think happened back there? Who's responsible?"

Miguel collapsed in a chair, his legs stretched out in front of him. She'd noticed the weight loss before, but his gaunt face and lanky appearance really hit her. Miguel had played baseball in college and had kept himself in peak condition throughout his navy SEAL training and beyond. The months in captivity had taken their toll on his body. What about his mind? How did anyone go through that without requiring psychological help to recover? Was that why the people in DC hadn't wanted him to leave?

He ran his knuckles along his jaw, which now sported a scruffy beard. "I don't think that was the government."

"You don't *think*? Would a government agency toss a Molotov cocktail into a child's bedroom?" She pressed her folded arms against her belly and the knots forming there.

"The FBI? No."

"But you weren't being debriefed by the FBI, were you? Or the CIA?"

"No."

"Would this…other agency do something like that?"

"That room in the front of the house could've been any room. Maybe Mikey wasn't the target."

She pushed off the counter and did a quick circle around the dumpy room. "That excuses them? They knew there was a child in the house. You said that's how you found out about Mikey— from their files."

He held up his hands. "I'm not excusing the

inexcusable, but it would be easier to believe this other agency tossed that Molotov cocktail into a house without targeting a child, but…"

"But what?"

"What would be their motive? They want me to come back, for sure, but they don't want to kill me."

"Then who?" Jennifer hunched her shoulders. "Who *would* want to kill you…or us?"

Miguel jumped from the chair and perched on the edge of the bed. He placed a hand on Mikey's back. "I'd never let anything happen to you or Mikey. You know that, don't you?"

"You didn't answer my question, Miguel. Who?"

"There's only one person I know who wants me dead."

Jennifer licked her lips. "You don't mean Vlad?"

Mikey stirred and flinched in his sleep, and Miguel rubbed a circle on his back.

How did he instinctively know what Mikey needed? As far as she knew, he hadn't been around small kids much. He'd been a younger brother, and while his older brother, Roberto, was married and had children, Miguel hadn't seen much of his niece and nephews.

"Vlad."

"That doesn't make sense either. Vlad had you, didn't he? You said you were captured and the rest of the team was killed while on a mission to find Vlad. It must've been his people who had you imprisoned."

"At that time, I was more valuable to Vlad alive. He probably thought he could lure the rest of my sniper team out and pick them off one by one."

"That didn't happen."

"My team thought I was dead. It almost worked once when Austin heard some chatter about Vlad's whereabouts."

"Austin Foley?"

"Yeah. He still thought I was dead, but Vlad's people were responsible for an IED that killed Austin's brother. He was all-in to track down Vlad, but the navy nixed the mission."

"Now that you're not useful to Vlad anymore, you think he's out to kill you? In Texas?"

"He has operatives working Stateside now. You know the incident at the JFK Library a few months ago?"

"That was Vlad?" She plopped down in the chair that Miguel had vacated. "He's built himself a terrorist network, hasn't he?"

"It wasn't just the attempt at the library. We destroyed a training camp he was running in Somalia, and he had entered into a deal with a Colombian drug cartel to exchange drugs for weapons and passage into the US."

"Oh, my God, Miguel. This is bad. And this is the man who's after you? After us?"

"I can't be certain because…" Miguel absently smoothed the pad of his thumb across a lock of Mikey's hair, over and over.

"Because what?"

"Something seemed off at the debriefing center."

"What do you mean by that?" The faraway look in Miguel's eyes had her digging her fingers into her upper arms. How much psychological counseling had he received after his imprisonment? Miguel had nerves of steel, but conditions like he'd experienced, even though he wouldn't tell her about them, would be enough to break anyone.

"What seemed off, Miguel?" She glided slowly across the room until she hovered above him, still seated on the edge of the bed.

"I felt like I was being held captive again."

"That's understandable." She dropped her hand to his shoulder and squeezed.

"I escaped the compound in Maryland just as surely as I escaped from my cell in Afghanistan." He threaded his fingers through hers and she felt the slight tremble of his hand. "Something wasn't right at that compound, Jennifer— something or someone."

"You're scaring me, Miguel." Was he imagining things? Paranoid? She untangled her fingers from his and stepped back, shooting a quick glance at Mikey.

A stab of guilt lanced her belly. Miguel wouldn't hurt his son. He'd been nothing but tender with him ever since he rescued him from that burning room—and that fire hadn't been the figment of his imagination.

His dark eyes flickered, and he pushed to his feet. "I don't want to scare you, Jen. Maybe I never should've come back into your life. I probably led the bad guys—whoever they are—right to your doorstep."

"That's not true." She pressed a hand to her hot cheek. "They'd already found me. They broke into my house. Th-they've been watching me."

His head jerked around. "How do you know that?"

"I just felt it, even before the break-in."

He curled a hand around her neck. "You need a safe place, you and Mikey."

A safe place? Away from him? "I have to finish out the school year. There are two more days of class this week and the fifth-grade promotion the day after tomorrow. I'm not going anywhere."

"I'll get you through the rest of the school year." He pulled her close and kissed her forehead. "Now you need to get to sleep. You and Mikey take the bed and I'll bunk here on the couch."

She drew her eyebrows over her nose. He

wasn't going to sleep with her his first night back? She'd dreamed of lying in his arms so many times over the past two years and now that she had him within her reach, he was slipping away.

Was it because he saw the doubt in her eyes?

He pressed his index finger between her eyes as if to flatten out her frown. "I'm not going to sleep. I'm going to keep watch over you and Mikey."

"You look tired, Miguel. You need to sleep, too."

"I've gone without a good, full night's sleep for so long now, I don't even know what I'm missing anymore." He pointed to the bathroom. "You first. Go brush your teeth and all that."

Ten minutes later when she came out of the bathroom, Miguel, sitting on the edge of the sofa, glanced up from his cell phone, his face drawn, his eyes hollow.

Jennifer forced a smile to her face and swallowed. "All yours."

He turned his phone facedown on the table beside the sofa and jumped to his feet. "Crawl into the bed next to Mikey. I'll be done in two minutes and then I'll keep watch over both of you."

As soon as the bathroom door closed behind him, she rushed to the phone, grabbing it before it could go to sleep. She tapped the display and the most recent text message came to life.

As she read the words from Josh Elliott, one of Miguel's sniper teammates, her heart did somersaults in her chest.

She was still clutching the phone when Miguel emerged from the bathroom, and she held it up to him, reciting the words she'd memorized.

"'Mole. Don't know how deep. Gunning for you—and Jen.'"

Chapter Four

A muscle in Miguel's jaw jumped. "You read my text?"

"That's all you have to say?" She waved the phone at him. "When were you going to tell me?"

"About the mole?" He ran a hand through his hair. "I just found out."

"I repeat. When were you going to tell me about it? Ever?" She tossed the phone against the back cushion of the sofa, and it bounced and landed on the floor. "You're not back twenty-four hours and you're already keeping things from me."

Heat burned in his chest, along with the guilt. "Jen, this is different."

"Really? Aren't you going to tell me that I'm better off not knowing for my own safety? Why don't you let me decide what's best for my own safety? Were you planning to leave me again *for my own safety*?"

Clasping the back of his neck, he bit the inside of his cheek. The thought had crossed his mind that with him out of the picture, Jen would be safe, but Josh's text indicated the mole was after Jennifer, too.

As she studied his face, her eyes grew round. "You were. You were going to leave us—me and Mikey."

In two steps, he ate up the distance between them and pulled her stiff body into his arms. "I'm never going to leave you again. Yeah, I did think maybe you'd be better off without me back in your life, but I learned to be selfish in captivity. I'm not gonna let you go—not now, not ever."

She struggled against him for a few seconds until he cupped her face in his hands and planted a desperate kiss against her lips. Then she seemed to go boneless in his arms, melting against his chest.

She pulled away from his kiss and whispered hoarsely in his ear, "Don't ever leave me again, Miguel. I almost died when they told me you were dead."

He massaged a circle on her back and rested his chin on top of her head, the honey-blond strands of her hair clinging to his beard.

She hooked one arm around his waist and slid the other hand up the front of his shirt, splaying her fingers across his bare chest. "Make it real. Let me know you're back."

Throwing a quick glance at his son's sleeping form, Miguel stepped back from Jennifer's searching hands. If he needed an excuse for not being intimate with his fiancée, that excuse lay in a flushed tumble on the bed. "Is this a good idea?"

Tugging at his shirt, she replied, "He's not even two. He's not going to know what's going on over here even if he does wake up. And he won't."

All his muscles tensed, but Miguel tried to put a smile on his face. "If you say so."

"I say so." She bunched his shirt in her hands and yanked it up. "Help me out here."

Holding his breath, Miguel pulled his shirt over his head.

Jennifer gasped.

Miguel crumpled his T-shirt in one fist. "Yeah, maybe this isn't such a good idea after all. I probably should've warned you."

Her fingertips traced the scars crisscrossing his chest. Then she nudged him with her hands to turn around.

"Not much better back there."

She smoothed her hands across the various wounds on his back, exploring them as if committing them to memory. "H-how did you ever survive this?"

"By thinking of this." He turned to face her and wrapped his hands around her waist.

He slanted his mouth across hers, slipping his tongue into her mouth, where it did a familiar tango with hers.

He could do this if he just maintained a certain level of control. He wouldn't allow himself to let go.

Jennifer wedged her fingers in the waistband of his jeans and yanked at his zipper.

"Mama." A wail quickly followed the single word.

Miguel jerked back from Jennifer. What had he been thinking? He could never maintain control with Jen.

She kissed Miguel's chest. "Let me settle him. I'll be right back."

She sat on the edge of the bed and a few minutes later Miguel joined her, kneeling on the floor.

Mikey rubbed his eyes and let out another wail. Jennifer pulled him into her lap. "It's okay, Mikey. We're in a hotel, but you're with Mama... and your daddy."

A knot twisted in Miguel's gut. He'd wanted to be a dad for so long, but the conditions couldn't be worse. "Do you think he's ready for that, Jen? Ready for me?"

"The sooner the better. Might as well get him used to the idea."

"Doesn't look as if he much likes the idea of a daddy."

Mikey's face had crumpled, and fresh tears rolled down his cheeks as he stared at his new-found father.

"He's probably having a delayed reaction to that explosion in his room and the fire. He hardly had time to react before you swooped in there to save him. Now he's waking up in a strange place." She shrugged.

"With a strange man."

"Not for long, Miguel. He'll adapt quickly. Kids do."

"We're not giving him much to adapt to—a motel room instead of his home, most of his clothes and toys ruined." He touched Mikey's little fist, curled around a lock of Jennifer's hair. "Has he had many men in his life?"

She sucked in a quick breath of air. "Dad and Mom have been to visit a few times, but Alicia's husband, Troy, has probably been the most prominent male in Mikey's life, since I see Alicia and Troy a few times a month."

Her words left a sour taste in his mouth. He didn't even like Troy, the husband of Jen's best friend, and that guy had a more important role in Mikey's life than he did.

Miguel met Mikey's watery gaze and winked. He supposed he should be feeling grateful that Troy was there for Mikey…and Jen.

Jennifer kissed the top of Mikey's head. "I'm

going to change his diaper and try to get him to go back to sleep."

"Can I watch? If I'm gonna be a dad, I'd better start learning the basics."

"Of course. Nothing to it." She scooted off the bed with Mikey clutched to her chest. Pointing to the corner where he'd stashed her bags, she said, "Bring me that green diaper bag. We'll do it here on the floor."

He strode to the corner and swept up the bag. He crouched beside her at the foot of the bed. "What do we need?"

"Changing pad in the side pocket, fresh diaper, wipes, a little tube of cream in the zipper pouch inside and a plastic grocery bag."

He pulled out all the items she'd requested and lined them up on the floor, holding the diaper in his hand. "This looks like a complicated operation."

"Only when he's squiggly." She grabbed Mikey's kicking feet and pressed a kiss on each sole. "I'm going to start potty training him in about six months. Alicia said boys are slower than girls, but Bella was potty trained at twenty-six months."

"If Bella can do it, Mikey can do it. Right, big guy?" Miguel poked Mikey's belly with his finger, and his son rewarded him with a giggle.

Jennifer made short work of the task, and let him secure the fresh diaper into place.

He wrapped up the soiled diaper in the plastic bag and put it in the bathroom trash. Then he washed his hands and put everything back in its place in the diaper bag.

Jennifer had returned to the bed with Mikey and curled up beside him. "He's still a little restless, so I'm going to cuddle with him until he falls asleep. Then we can get back to what we were doing. You got me all hot changing that diaper. Nothing sexier than a man changing a diaper."

He shook his head. "That's weird. Is the TV going to bother you?"

"Just keep it low."

Miguel pulled his T-shirt back on and settled on the couch, clicking on the TV. He scanned through the channels until he found a news program and then glanced at Jennifer, her eyes closed.

Bending forward, he retrieved his phone from the floor and texted Josh, asking if he had any more details about the mole.

Josh responded quickly and Miguel read the text with growing dread. Josh had had some contact with Vlad's people on Josh's recent Stateside assignment, protecting the daughter of the drug kingpin Hector De Santos. Vlad's guys had implied they had someone on the inside, and Josh had no reason to doubt that, at least he hadn't wanted to bet against it.

Miguel clenched his jaw as he thought about Vlad, their nemesis. They'd been on Vlad's trail when Miguel had been captured. He'd had a long time to think about a mole then.

Where had the SEAL team gotten the intel about Vlad's location in those caves in Afghanistan? Through the Vlad task force? Was it just bad information, or was it very, very good information planted for the SEAL team, and him as the sniper, to walk right into an ambush?

Almost eighteen months later and after his escape from his captors, the CIA didn't seem all that interested in finding out. Could this mole have infiltrated the top echelons? The task force itself?

Josh ended their text exchange with a curt directive. Watch your back.

Miguel tossed his phone on the cushion next to him, his gaze shifting to Jennifer, her body curved around Mikey's, both of them sound asleep.

Miguel pulled his gun from beneath the cushion of the couch and hunched forward, watching the blue light from the TV flicker over Jennifer and Mikey. Instead of weakening him, his captivity had made him strong, hard—maybe too hard to be a family man.

But not too hard to protect them with every inch of his life.

A LITTLE HAND grabbed her nose, and Jennifer opened one eye while puffing a strand of hair from her face. "What are you doing, rascal?"

"Wake up, Mommy."

"I'm awake." She rolled to her back and raised her head. "Tell me you got some sleep on that couch."

Miguel, showered and fully dressed down to a pair of scuffed cowboy boots, pushed up from the couch where he'd been perched. "I slept some."

"How long has this one been awake?" She jerked her thumb at Mikey.

"Not long. Woke up, stared at me for a few minutes and proceeded to tweak your nose." He stretched. "If I'd known it was that easy to wake you up, I would've used that method years ago."

She ran her tongue along her teeth. "I remember how you used to wake me up…and I distinctly prefer your method."

He gave her a tight smile. "What time do you have to get to school?"

She swallowed. Except for their desperate kisses last night, Miguel didn't seem all that interested in picking up where they'd left off. "I have to be there at eight, but I need to drop off

Mikey at his day care about fifteen minutes before that."

"It's close, the day care?"

"It's a few blocks from the school." She lifted Mikey and swung him over her head. "Can you watch him while I take a shower?"

Miguel's eyes widened as his gaze darted around the hotel room. "This room isn't baby-proofed. Is it safe?"

Hooking Mikey on one hip and placing her hand on the other, she surveyed the room. "Don't let him rip up the brochures on the credenza, keep the remote out of his picky little paws and, by all means, keep him away from the electrical outlets and the minibar. Otherwise, I think you're good. I'll change his diaper before I hit the shower."

"Let me do that." He took a step forward, holding out his arms. "I need the practice."

She cocked her head to one side. "You sure would've come in handy these past eighteen months."

A shade dropped over Miguel's dark eyes and she bit her bottom lip. Miguel's captivity had made him even more intense, but she couldn't contain her own elation. Since his return yesterday, despite the challenges they faced, the heavy, dark cloud that had been following her around for two years had dissipated into fairy dust.

"I'm sorry, Jen."

She went to him and placed Mikey against his chest, wrapping her arms around both of them. "Dear God, you have nothing to be sorry about, Miguel."

"I should've never volunteered for that assignment."

"I thought you didn't have a choice. Besides, you did what you thought was right. You always do." She brushed her lips across Mikey's soft hair and then pressed them against the stubble on Miguel's jaw. "Diaper duty for you."

She spun around, blindly lurching for the bathroom, tears blurring her vision. When she slammed the door behind her, she hunched over the vanity and peered at her reflection. The woman who gazed back at her had dropped ten years since yesterday.

She knew she couldn't expect Miguel to be the same person he was when he left her two years ago, but had his feelings for her changed? No. He'd told her she'd been the one keeping him strong, keeping him alive.

Did he really think she cared about the scars on his body? She snorted as she cranked on the water for the shower. Even though he'd lost a little muscle as a prisoner, he still had the hottest body she'd ever had the pleasure of exploring—scars or no scars. And she planned to do more exploration, damn it.

Maybe having Mikey in the same room had scared him off. She tipped her head back and let the warm spray course through her hair. He sure seemed eager to make up for lost time and learn everything he could about toddler care. Alicia's husband, Troy, had probably changed a grand total of ten diapers in the past two years of Bella's life.

The bathroom door burst open and Miguel's voice rose above the water. "I think I need some help out here."

Grabbing the edge of the shower curtain, Jennifer peeked into the bathroom at Miguel looming in the doorway with a squiggling Mikey tucked under one arm. "What happened?"

"First, he wouldn't let me put his clothes on after I changed his diaper. Then he started jumping on the bed. When I tried to grab him, he crawled off the edge and fell on the floor." Miguel took a deep breath. "I think he's okay."

"Well, these are the terrible toddler years." She pointed to her soapy head. "I'll be done in a few minutes." She grinned at Miguel's panicked expression. "Welcome to fatherhood. You'll think of something."

She whipped the shower curtain back in place and stuck her head under the water to rinse. When she finished her shower, she dropped the towel on the floor and slipped into some clean underwear.

She opened the bathroom door a crack and put her eye to the space. Two lumps, one large and one small, moved beneath the covers of the bed.

She swung open the door. "Everything okay?"

Miguel lifted one edge of the blanket. "We're under the ocean waves here, swimming."

Mikey's muffled voice echoed Miguel's. "Swimming."

"In your diaper?"

Mikey wriggled from beneath the covers. "Swimming."

"I see that, but now you have to get dressed so Mommy can drop you off at Ms. Lori's room."

"Does he need breakfast?"

"They feed him there."

"What about you?"

"If I get moving and leave a little early, I can pick up something on the way."

"We." Miguel shrugged off the blanket and held Mikey's arm as he clambered off the bed. "I'm taking you to school, and I'm picking you both up."

She nodded, a pinprick of fear needling the back of her neck. "What are you going to do all day or at least until noon? We get out early today since the kids just have graduation practice."

"I'm going to do some research."

"On?"

"Moles."

AFTER THEY DROPPED off Mikey and picked up some breakfast burritos, Miguel parked around the corner from the school.

Jennifer peeled back the yellow paper from her burrito and pointed to the bag. "Any hot sauce in there?"

"Thought I saw some." Miguel plunged his hand into the bag and pulled out two packets of hot sauce. He ripped one open with his teeth and handed it to her.

"Who do you think broke into my house and firebombed it? Same group for both actions?" She squeezed the red sauce onto the end of her burrito and took a bite.

"Not sure." He raised his hand and ticked off the recent events on his fingers. "You think someone's been following you. Someone broke into your place and planted those bugs. Someone threw a Molotov cocktail into your house, but it wasn't a big one."

"Yeah, I feel so much better that someone threw a fiery rag in a glass bottle into my son's bedroom, but it was just a little, bitty one."

Miguel dabbed at a spot of hot sauce on his chin. "What I meant was that act could've been more of an attempt to warn and not kill."

"It could've killed." The hot sauce burned in her belly. "It could've killed Mikey."

"I know." He grabbed her hand. "I'm just trying to figure out motivation here. Is it the CIA trying to scare me back to Maryland or is it some terrorist cell trying to kill me?"

"And us."

Miguel's jaw tightened. "Maybe I never should've come back to you."

"We've been through this already. Before you even got to Austin, someone was following me and bugging my house."

"Probably just because they knew I'd return here. If I'd never come back, they probably would've lost interest in you and continued their search for me."

She dropped her burrito and dug her fingers into the denim covering his thigh. "Do you think you could've kept your return from me? I'm sure I would've found out somehow, and then nothing would've kept me from your side."

Drawing her toward him, he kissed her with his spicy lips. "I love you, Jen, more than anything, but that means keeping you safe."

"Yeah, yeah. I've heard that line before." She cupped his jaw flicking her fingers through his longish hair. "This is no military cut, sailor."

"They weren't offering and I wasn't asking. Had more important issues on my mind."

She glanced at her cell phone. "I have one more question before I head off to class. How could one mole in the intel community get to you?"

He jerked his thumb at the laptop stashed in

the backseat. "That's what I'm going to try to find out."

"Can Josh Elliott help you?" She crumpled up the waxy paper around the rest of her burrito and tossed it into the bag at Miguel's feet.

"No. He's headed out for another deployment. He had a little time off after his last assignment. Guess he met a woman."

"Josh?" Miguel's sniper teammate was more intense than Miguel. "I hope she's tough as nails."

"She's..." Miguel shrugged. "I hope so, too. I'm going to be waiting right here for you at noon, and then we'll pick up Mikey."

"And then?"

"We should find another house. Mikey can't stay in a motel forever."

"Tomorrow is the last day of school. Let's deal with it then."

A bell rang in the distance, and Miguel raised his eyebrows. "Are you late, teacher?"

"That's the first bell. I'm not late until the second bell." She kissed him again just because she could and he was inches away from her. "Noon."

Before she turned the corner, she glanced back at the car and waved. She still felt like she was moving through some crazy dream. Miguel alive, back home—and their lives in danger. When would they catch a break?

She had no time to pop into the teachers'

lounge like she usually did, so she headed straight for her classroom.

The first bell had called the kids to class, and they jostled and nudged each other as they lined up in the hallway outside the door.

"You're almost in middle school. Behave yourselves." She jingled her key chain at them and then opened the door.

"What're we doing today, Ms. Lynch?"

"I must've told you a hundred times, Chase." She dropped her bag on the floor and nudged it under her desk with her toe. "Cleaning up the room. You guys are going to take all your stuff home, projects, papers, supplies, and then we're going to walk to the high school to run through the promotion ceremony."

The morning passed quickly, and at ten thirty Jennifer got her class ready for the walk to the high school. As she gathered the kids in the hallway, Olivia sidled up next to her.

"What happened at your house last night? I heard there was a fire."

"That news spread quickly." Jennifer snapped her fingers. "Girls, stop talking. There are classes in session across the hall."

"Are you and Mikey okay?"

"We're fine. M-my friend discovered it quickly, got us out of the house and called 9-1-1."

"Thank goodness. When you didn't make it

to the teachers' lounge this morning, I got worried. Do you have a place to stay?"

"Motel for now. I'll start looking for a new place soon. I was done with that place anyway."

"It's a good thing it's the end of the school year." Olivia took Jennifer's arm. "One more day until freedom."

Freedom? Jennifer had been feeling a noose tightening around her neck ever since Miguel appeared—no, that wasn't fair. She'd been feeling that noose even before. She just hadn't understood its significance.

Just like they had the day before, the fifth-grade teachers herded their students through the park and across the street to the high school. The school had reserved its auditorium for their practice.

Once inside, the students were assigned a place in line alphabetically. The teachers gathered in the back while the principal and vice principal ran the kids through their paces.

Olivia took a sip from her coffee cup. "Are you and Mikey still going to visit your sister in San Francisco this summer?"

"Maybe." Olivia knew all about her dead navy SEAL fiancé. When would she be able to tell everyone the good news about Miguel? She was pretty tired of being the poor, young fiancée, left to raise a child by herself.

She wanted to shout the news from the rooftops. She wanted to tell Troy that Mikey no longer needed a father figure—he had his own father.

Jennifer sighed. "You still going out to visit the in-laws?"

"God, yes, for two long weeks."

A buzzing sound had Olivia patting her pockets. "It's not mine."

Jennifer reached for her purse hanging over the back of a chair in the last row of the auditorium and scrambled for her cell phone in the side pocket.

Her heart did a little flip when she saw the number for Mikey's day care. She held up one finger to Olivia. "Excuse me a minute. I have to take this."

"Hello?"

"Oh, Jennifer. I—I…" Franny, the owner of the day care, dragged in a ragged breath. "First of all, let me assure you that Mikey is safe."

The blood rushed to Jennifer's head all at once, and she grabbed the edge of the seat. "What does that mean? What happened?"

"Mikey's fine and we already called the police."

"The police? Franny, tell me what happened."

"A man broke into the center, into Ms. Lori's room. Jen, he tried to take Mikey."

Chapter Five

Jennifer gulped and pressed two fingers to her throbbing temple. "Where is Mikey now?"

"He's in my office with me. We're waiting for the police right now."

Shifting the phone away from her mouth, Jennifer tapped Olivia's arm and said, "I have to leave. Mikey's okay, but something happened at his day care. Tell Sandra I'll be gone the rest of the day."

Olivia's eyes grew round. "Go, go. I'll get your class back to the school and dismiss them."

As Jennifer hustled from the auditorium, she continued with Franny. "What happened? What do you mean someone tried to take him? Was it someone who tried to sign him out and pretend I sent him?"

Had Miguel tried to pick up his son, not realizing the security measures in place at the day care?

"I mean take, Jen, as in forcibly try to remove him from the center." Franny released a little sob.

A blast of adrenaline shot through Jennifer's body and she quickened her pace back to the school. "Are you sure Mikey's okay?"

"He's fine, sitting here having a snack. I don't know what we would've done if that other man hadn't charged into the play area and challenged the man who had Mikey."

"What? Another man?"

"As the man ran into the playground with Mikey under his arm, another guy leaped over the fence and knocked the kidnapper down. He got Mikey away from the man and handed him over to us. The kidnapper ran and the last I saw of Mikey's protector, he was going after him."

Mikey's protector? It had to be Miguel. He'd saved his son's life twice in two days.

Jennifer's heart was still beating erratically by the time she jogged the two blocks to Mikey's day care. When she got there, a police cruiser was stationed out front.

She bolted through the front gate and ran to the play yard, where two cops were talking to Franny and Lori. Panic stabbed the back of her skull when she didn't see Mikey with them.

"Where's Mikey?"

Franny hugged her. "He's back in Ms. Lori's room. Ms. Tina is watching the class. We thought it best not to isolate him from the other kids to get things back to normal for him. Is that okay?"

Jennifer clung to Franny for a few seconds before nodding. "Yes."

One of the officers stepped forward. "Ms. Lynch, I'm Officer Grady. The teachers were telling us that there are no custody disputes or family issues, is that correct?"

"That's right."

"And the father is...?"

"Deceased."

"His family?"

Jennifer blinked. This cop would have a field day with Miguel's family, but she already knew who was behind this attempted abduction, and it wasn't Miguel's brother, Roberto, or any of Roberto's enemies. "Mikey's paternal relatives are not involved in his life."

"Do they wanna be?" The officer chewed on the end of his pen. "Kidnappings like this usually end up being family members."

"Not in this case."

"What about the man who stopped the abduction." The other officer turned to Franny. "Was he a parent?"

"No, never saw him before." Franny shook her head so that her long, gray braid flicked back and forth.

Jennifer sucked in her bottom lip. Would Miguel want to be outed to these police officers?

Probably not. He didn't seem to know whom to trust, outside of his sniper team. She wouldn't put him at risk now.

Jennifer pressed a hand against the knots in her belly. "Maybe he was just a passerby who saw what was going on. I'm going to see my son."

She broke away from the group and entered the building. She had to tiptoe through the infant area to get to the toddler classroom. After all the excitement, most of the babies had conked out and were nestled in their bassinets.

Jennifer poked her head around the doorway into the toddler room and waved at Mikey, who was sitting at a table playing with blocks of different shapes and colors.

He waved a red square at her, a big grin on his face, punctuated by a few cookie crumbs.

Rolling her shoulders, she took a deep breath and plastered a smile on her face. "Hello, big boy."

"Hi, Mama."

She swooped in and lifted him from the plastic chair. She hugged him so tightly, he squirmed in her arms. "Are you having fun?"

"Yes." He put the corner of the block in his mouth. "Red square."

"That's right. Good job. Are you ready to go home?"

Mikey's little face crumpled and he showed her his elbow. "Boo-boo. I fell."

Tears stung the backs of her eyes while she kissed her son's scraped elbow. "I heard. Are you okay?"

Mikey put up his fists. "Boom, boom. The mans were fighting."

She clasped her hands over Mikey's fists and pressed her lips against his knuckles. Had he recognized Miguel? Had the teachers and the police asked him anything about the other man?

"I heard about the fight. You can tell me all about it when we get home, okay?"

"Policemans?"

"Yes, we can see the police officer again before we leave." She didn't know exactly how they'd leave, since Miguel had her car. She didn't want to call him to pick them up in case the day-care teachers recognized him.

She collected Mikey's things from Tina and walked back out to the play yard, squinting in the midday sun.

The police officer who'd been questioning the teachers had put away his notebook and the other seemed to be scouring the rubber surface of the playground for clues.

Officer Grady asked, "Ah, Ms. Lynch. How's your son?"

"He's fine, thanks." She approached the group, holding Mikey against her side. "He wanted to say goodbye to you."

"Bye-bye, Mikey." The officer waved. "Let

us know if you think of anyone who would do this, Ms. Lynch. I've already asked the teachers to call if the man who interrupted the...ah...incident comes back. We'd sure like to talk to him."

The officer searching the ground popped up, holding a white napkin in his hand. He held it up, the bright letters of the fast-food place where she and Miguel had eaten that morning blazing yellow and orange against the white backdrop. "Does this belong here?"

Franny sniffed. "We don't allow fast food at our day care."

"That place isn't far from here. It could've come from anyone's pocket." Jennifer lifted and dropped her shoulders quickly. "It might even be mine since I ate there this morning."

The eyes of the officer holding the napkin narrowed. "Is that right?"

As the heat crept into her cheeks, Jennifer rested her face against Mikey's head. "Maybe it fell out of my purse. It's not much, is it?"

"Maybe, maybe not, but it's something." He whipped out a plastic bag and placed the napkin inside. "I'm sure you're happy we found something."

"Of course, and I'm going to talk to Mikey tonight to see if he'll tell me anything." She patted Mikey's head against her shoulder. "D-did he tell you anything?"

Officer Grady answered, "I asked him a few

questions, but he's pretty young. We didn't expect much from him."

"Maybe I can find out something tonight."

"If so, let us know." The suspicious officer with the napkin pressed his card into her hand, even though Officer Grady had already given her his card earlier. "Don't go anywhere, Ms. Lynch."

"For how long?" She glanced at the card before pocketing it. "I'm a teacher and tomorrow is the last day of school. We have vacation plans."

"Just keep us posted, so we know where to reach you—in case something comes up."

"I'll do that." She hugged Franny again. "Thanks for everything."

"I'm afraid we didn't do much. If we ever locate that Good Samaritan, you can thank him yourself."

She would, personally.

Readjusting her bag over one shoulder and Mikey's bag over the other, she walked through the gate and landed in the parking lot, looking both ways. As she started making her way back to the school, she pulled out her cell phone and called Miguel.

He picked up after a half a ring. "Thank God. Is Mikey okay? Are you okay?"

"We're both fine. It was you, wasn't it? The man who saved Mikey?"

"Make a right at the first block. I'm parked

across the street from the park. Did you tell the police anything about me, about your hunch?"

"Of course not. I know you're trying to keep a low profile." She cranked her head around to make sure the police were still at the day care and then veered to the right.

Before she could utter another word, her car rolled backward on the street and idled next to her, Miguel at the wheel. She opened the back door and secured Mikey in his car seat. Then she slid into the passenger seat next to Miguel and slammed the door.

"Why are they after Mikey?"

"Because they're after me."

"But you don't even know who it is, do you?" She gripped her knees with both hands, tension lacing her shoulders. "Are you trying to tell me the CIA is going to kidnap a child, an American child from a day care center, to bring a navy SEAL into line?"

"I told you, Jen—" he wheeled around the corner and pulled up to a signal "—someone has infiltrated the Vlad task force. That person may be calling the shots or maybe has gone rogue. And then again…the people who just tried to take Mikey may not be with US intelligence at all."

Her nails dug into the fabric of her slacks. "I don't know which prospect is worse—a rogue CIA agent or a terrorist group."

Mikey shouted from the backseat, "Boom, boom. Mans fighting."

Miguel's brows shot up and he reached into the backseat to squeeze the toe of Mikey's light-up sneakers. "That's right, big guy. Your daddy had to take care of some business."

Mikey rewarded him with a big grin and started kicking the back of Jennifer's seat.

"Great. He's getting all aggressive." She turned and cinched Mikey's ankle above his sock. "Stop kicking, Mikey."

He gave the backseat one more shot from his toe, and then started singing.

"I'm sorry he had to be a part of that fight, but there's no other way I would've been able to get him out of that man's grasp—unless I pulled a gun, and I wasn't about to do just that."

"I'm sorry, Miguel." She brought her hand to the base of her throat. "I know you did what you had to do. If you hadn't wrestled Mikey from that man…"

"I wish I hadn't lost him, but he got away when I grabbed Mikey."

"Tell me what happened. Why were you at the day care?"

"After I dropped you off, I started thinking about the day care and how easy it would be for someone to walk right in there."

"You already figured Mikey was in danger?"

"If someone didn't care about firebombing

your house with a child inside, I knew we were dealing with some hard-core people."

Her jaw tightened and she felt as if she might break into a thousand brittle pieces. "You went back to the day care?"

"I parked around the corner and took up watch across the street."

"Across the street? There are houses across the street."

"I saw a husband and wife leaving for work, so I hopped their fence and tucked myself into a corner next to a tree. I knew nobody could see me from the street."

She studied his profile, more angular than she'd remembered. "How long did you sit there?"

"Dropped you off at eight, slipped into that yard around eight thirty and the guy showed up at the day care around eleven—about two and a half hours."

"In the same position for two and a half hours?"

He quirked one brow at her. "You forget what I do, Jen?"

"Yeah, I suppose that's nothing for you." She grabbed his forearm. "I'm so glad you were there. I knew it was you as soon as Franny told me a man had jumped in to rescue Mikey. When did you notice what was happening?"

"As soon as the guy walked up to the day care,

my sensors went on high alert. He just had a look. Didn't look like a dad."

"Really?" She glanced in the backseat at a drowsy Mikey and turned down the radio. They didn't need to drown out their words now. "Dads come in all shapes and sizes."

"I know. I guess I'm stereotyping, but this guy looked tense, alert."

"Takes one to know one."

Miguel grimaced. "When I saw him, I jumped onto the sidewalk. It didn't take him long to come barreling out of that building with Mikey under one arm and a gaggle of teachers on his tail."

"Maybe this will prompt the day care to put some barrier between the open front door and the kids."

"I'm not sure any barrier would've stopped this man. Nothing but a bullet would've stopped him…or a well-placed fist."

"That's what you did? Knocked him out?"

"Like I said. I was afraid to come in with a gun blazing. I tackled him, and he held onto Mikey as he fell. I was able to apply enough pressure that he had to release Mikey. I rolled over to shield Mikey, and that's when the man got up and started running. I think he saw the gun in my waistband, and that made his decision for him."

"You went after him?" Her knees had started bouncing in some sort of delayed reaction.

"Once I secured Mikey with his teacher, I chased him. I saw him go around the corner, but he must've had a car waiting because he just disappeared when I rounded that corner."

"H-how was Mikey when it happened?"

He took her hand. "He was scared, crying. I don't think he recognized me or realized it was me. His teachers did a good job of calming him down. I don't know that he even realized what was going on, but the violence had to have frightened him." He slammed a fist against the steering wheel. "It's just that type of violence I want to protect him from."

"I think you had a good excuse, Miguel." She traced a finger over his knuckles. "Don't be so hard on yourself. My God, you saved his life."

"Jen, we're going to have to leave here."

"Here?"

"Austin. We have to leave Austin."

She pulled on her earlobe. "I figured we would."

"At first I thought it would be good enough if I left." He held up his hand as she opened her mouth. "Not forever. I would've been back once I resolved this…problem. But now they're onto you and Mikey. It's not going to matter if I stay with you or not. If I don't stay with you, I have no way of protecting you—and you need protection."

He'd hit the freeway and took the exit back to the motel.

"I'm glad you see it that way because I'm not letting you out of my sight, Miguel Estrada."

He squealed into the parking slot in front of the motel room. "Pack your stuff, and we'll return to the house so you can pick up a few more things."

"Everything is still pretty much packed from our escape from the house. I'll go through our things tomorrow after school to see what else I can salvage."

He cut the engine and stared straight ahead, gripping the steering wheel. "You don't get it. We need to leave right now."

She jerked her head toward him. "Now? I can't leave now. I have one more day of school."

"You said it's graduation or promotion or whatever tomorrow."

"It is, but I still need to be there."

"Are your grades done?"

"Yes."

"End-of-the-year party, picnics, conferences all over."

"Yes."

"Then you can leave—and you have to."

"I suppose I can call in sick." She eyed the cell phone in her lap. "I hate to miss the ceremony."

"I'm sure you do, but Mikey's safety is more important, isn't it?"

"Of course, if you think…"

"Jen, someone found out where he attended day care, knew when he'd be there, knew there was light security and attempted to snatch him from beneath the teachers' noses. I think we need to leave—now."

"All right." She released a deep breath. "Where are we going to go?"

"I think I have a plan. Can you just get your stuff ready right now? I need to turn in my rental car. We'll get back to your house to get your things, and maybe you can call a packing and moving service to have the rest of the house boxed up and moved to storage. Is that possible?"

"I can do that. In fact, the management company would be thrilled if I took care of that, and then the insurance adjusters could move in and do their assessments of the damage."

He flipped the door handle and stopped, glancing at her frozen in the passenger seat. "Are you okay? I know this is all a huge shock and disruption to your life."

"I guess I'm just being a princess." She folded her arms. "Remember when you used to tease me that I came from a perfect world with a white picket fence and 2.5 kids?"

"I was a cocky idiot because that's exactly the world I want with you right now, except maybe we could have three kids instead of two and a half."

She gurgled and punched his arm. "I knew what you meant though. I'd never faced any adversity growing up. Mom had even been clean and sober for a few years before she had me and my sister. For a few seconds there I was just wishing that your homecoming could've been different."

"There's nothing wrong with that. I wish it could've been different, but I'll take what I can get."

"So will I—I'll take what I can get if it means having you." She flung open the door. "So let's get going."

As she ducked into the backseat to retrieve a sleeping Mikey, Miguel stood guard over them as if he thought a car might come screeching up at this very minute—and maybe he was right.

He hustled them into the room, bolted the door and took out his weapon. "I'll pack up what little I have. We can buy anything Mikey needs on the road."

She settled Mikey in the middle of the bed and went into the bathroom to collect her toiletries. She called over her shoulder. "You said you had a plan? What is it? Where are we going?"

Miguel loomed in the doorway of the bathroom. "Desperate times call for desperate measures. I thought we could go to Roberto's."

Jennifer dropped her bottle of shampoo in the tub. "You thought we'd be safe with a criminal?"

Chapter Six

Miguel gripped the doorjamb, his knuckles white. "I think it's our only option right now."

"You're kidding." Jennifer bent forward and swept up the shampoo bottle. She waved it at him. "You avoided Roberto like the plague. You even had the bright idea to break up with me to protect me from your family. Now we're running straight into the lion's den?"

"It's different now. Roberto's different."

"Oh, right. He gave up committing petty crimes with your father to be some kind of fixer. I'm sure he's completely legitimate." She snorted and fired the bottle of shampoo into her bag.

"It's because he lives on the edge that I thought he could help you—us. Think about it. Security is so tight at his compound, I doubt the mail carrier even gets through."

"It feels like we'd be swapping one dangerous situation for another."

"It's not my first choice." He ran a hand through his hair. "But I'm not sure where else Mikey and you would be safe from these people. There's a mole, Jen. I don't know who to trust. I'm not even sure I can trust Ariel."

"Who's Ariel?" She tipped her head to the side. "I thought all your sniper buddies were male."

"I honestly don't know if Ariel is a male or female, but she—or he—has been running the show in regards to Vlad. She coordinated three different missions Stateside, and Austin, Slade and Josh all worked with her. Josh told me to contact her."

"But you think she could be the mole?"

"I don't know." He stepped aside to let her out of the bathroom with her toiletries hastily tossed in a bag. "Maybe it's not her, but it could be someone close to her. I don't trust anyone. That's the problem. The CIA or the FBI might offer you protection at this point, but how do I know it's not some trap?"

Dropping her toiletry bag on top of her suitcase, Jennifer sighed. "If you can't trust the FBI, who can you trust?"

"Roberto."

"The criminal."

"The fixer."

"Can he fix this?" She spread her arms out to her sides to encompass the dumpy motel room.

"He can keep you and Mikey safe. I know that."

"Will he want to?"

Miguel's eye twitched. "My big brother has been wanting to get back in my good graces for some time. I cut him out of my life when he chose to go down the wrong path with Dad. I'd always looked up to him. Since he was ten years older than I was, he always did play the protector. He always took the brunt of Dad's anger to shield me. I even think that's why Roberto joined our father in his criminal pursuits—to keep the pressure off me."

She crossed the small room in two steps to stand in front of him and brushed her hands over his face. "I know that, and I know how hard it was for you to disown him. Is this some kind of plan to make it up to him?"

He cupped the back of her head and pressed his forehead against hers. "I'm not driven by emotions like that, Jen. This is a cold, hard business deal. He can offer protection, and we're going to take advantage of that."

She gave him a quick kiss before breaking away. "I don't even know where he lives these days."

"In California. Palm Springs."

"We're going to Palm Springs for the summer?"

"It could be worse." He glanced at the door of the room and the knots tightened in his gut. They'd been here too long. "Let's get moving. Is Mikey a good traveler in the car?"

"The motion puts him to sleep, but we'll have to make plenty of stops. Toddlers cannot stay strapped in a car seat for long stretches of time."

"We can do that. I've got a bum hip that I need to keep stretching, so I'll be right there with Mikey. Maybe this road trip will give me an opportunity to get to know him under somewhat normal circumstances. You think?"

"You've saved his life twice. I'd say you're already his hero."

Miguel glanced at his sleeping son, sprawled out in the middle of the bed, and his chest tightened. "I want to be more than his hero. I want to be his father."

Two HOURS LATER, after collecting the rest of Jennifer's belongings, turning in Miguel's rental car and renting a storage unit, they hit the road.

For the first hour in the car, Mikey called out all the words he knew in his developing vocabulary, including *Daddy*. When Mikey first tried out that word from the backseat, Miguel got a lump in his throat.

Mikey finally got tired of the game and after

a quick stop for dinner and a diaper change, he drifted off to sleep.

Jennifer grabbed her soda from the cupholder. "Are you sure you don't want me to drive for a while?"

"I'm used to staying awake and alert. I can handle it."

"How far are we going tonight?"

"It's another six hours to El Paso. I figured I can drive straight through."

"That means we won't get there until almost two in the morning." Jennifer tapped on the digital clock display on her dashboard. "Where are we going to sleep?"

"Do you want to look up a hotel on your phone? Find someplace where we can check in late." He nudged his wallet on the console between them. "There's a black credit card in there. Use that to secure the room."

Jennifer retrieved her phone from her purse, dropped it in her lap and flipped through his wallet. She clicked on the dome light and held the card beneath the soft yellow glow.

"Raymond Garcia." She peered at him over the edge of the card. "That's you?"

"Yeah, but I'm replacing that ID as soon as I can. It was assigned to me at the debriefing center in Maryland and I'm the only one who's supposed to know that identity, but I have my doubts. I wouldn't even use it, but we can't use your cards and we really need to get a place for the night."

"Does that mean I get to be Mrs. Garcia for tonight?"

"Absolutely."

"Good." She started tapping the display on her phone. "At least we can pretend we're married since we missed out on that other wedding."

He reached over and squeezed her knee. He'd already put her through hell, and it hadn't ended yet. Would it ever?

He almost hadn't returned to her, thinking she'd be safer without him in her life, but when he discovered she'd had Mikey and that the FBI was already monitoring some suspicious activity surrounding Jennifer, he didn't have a choice.

His hands curled around the steering wheel. He'd never forgive the FBI for keeping the knowledge of his son from him. A man shouldn't have to discover he's a father by reading it in a stolen file by flashlight in the dead of night.

Jennifer finished speaking into the phone and then ended the call. "I got us a room just outside of El Paso, twenty-four-hour check-in, and they'll even have a crib in the room for us."

"Sounds good. Why don't you get some sleep? We'll be on the road for a while."

"I cannot sleep in a car, sitting upright—not even slouched over. I'll keep you company. Besides—" she ran her fingertips across his knuckles "—I feel like we haven't talked at all. I mean really talked."

"You're right. We haven't." He'd been so damned worried Jen would want to know the details of his captivity—and he couldn't go there, wouldn't go there with her. "Tell me everything about your pregnancy. I want to know when you found out, how you found out, how you felt. Was it physically easy for you? Did you have cravings? Who held your hand when you got sick or when you were scared? Who was there for you when Mikey was born, when I should've been?"

She sucked in a sharp breath at his last question. Then she tucked one leg under her body and took a sip of her soda.

"I found out a few weeks after you deployed."

"I'm sorry," he whispered into the darkness, the words sounding hollow and inadequate.

Sniffling, she swiped a hand across her face. "Don't be. It was the best news I could've gotten—to have you still with me while you were away."

"It must've been a shock. It's not like we were planning to start a family this early."

"A happy shock. A welcome shock." She brushed her hands together as if dismissing the sadness of the past. "And I found out the usual way—pregnancy test from the local drug store.

I danced around the room when I saw the double lines."

"I can picture that."

"What else did you want to know?" She ticked off the answers on her fingers. "Easy pregnancy. Called my mom and my sister, Hannah, when I got scared or had questions. Alicia was my rock. Mom and Hannah were with me in the delivery room."

"Do you have lots of pictures of Mikey? I saw the ones from the house that you packed up."

"Tons. I'll show you more on my computer tomorrow, if we have some time at the hotel before we hit the road." She tapped her phone to bring up the GPS. "How much longer to Palm Springs from El Paso?"

"Probably another ten hours. We'll head for Tucson from El Paso, but I don't plan to spend the night anywhere else. We can get to my brother's place by six o'clock tomorrow if we power through."

She jerked her thumb over her shoulder. "I think that depends on Mikey. If he gets fussy, we'll have to stop."

"Got it. Tell me more. Tell me everything."

The hours and the road flew by as Jennifer told him about his son. He drank it all in, absorbing it into his very marrow.

Her speech began to slow down and slur until she gave up and rested her head against the window.

"Do you want a blanket from the backseat to put beneath your head?"

"I'm not sleeping."

"Maybe not, but you might be more comfortable."

"I'm not sleeping."

He brushed a lock of hair from her cheek and squeezed her shoulder. "Okay, Jen."

Within minutes, her breathing deepened and her head sunk closer to her shoulder.

Miguel adjusted the rearview mirror to peek at Mikey. Like mother, like son.

He traveled the rest of the way across Texas with his own thoughts to keep him company. He was accustomed to that, too. His captors had kept him in solitary most of the time. He didn't want to think about the men who'd shared his space from time to time or what had happened to them when they'd been dragged out of the cell never to return.

Now he had to protect his family from that evil at home, but it was worse. At least in captivity, he'd known his enemy. Here he couldn't be sure.

He knew he could trust Roberto though. His older brother might be a ruthless man, but he needed Roberto's ruthlessness on his side right now.

By the time they reached the outskirts of

El Paso, Jennifer had woken up from her restless sleep.

"We're here already?"

"According to your phone's GPS, the hotel should be off the next exit."

She twisted around and tucked Mikey's blanket around his legs. "Did he wake up?"

"Not once, but then you told me that you could get him to sleep as a baby by taking him for a ride in the car."

She tilted her head at him. "I did tell you that, didn't I?"

He flicked on the turn signal, although the nearest car on the road had just passed him. The GPS directed him to turn right, and he spotted the lighted hotel sign up ahead.

The check-in for Mr. and Mrs. Garcia was smooth, since he had an Arizona driver's license to match his credit card.

The chipper clerk assured them the crib had been installed in the room while rolling a dubious eye at Mikey, who'd awakened with a vengeance.

Jennifer smiled at the woman. "I'm sure he'll be back to sleep soon."

When they got to their room on the second floor, Miguel parked their bags in the corner and stretched. "That wasn't so bad."

"You're crazy. You must be tight after driving for six straight hours." Jennifer came up behind him and dug the fingers of one hand into the knots in the back of his neck. "How's that hip?"

Seconds later, Mikey, hooked on Jennifer's hip, patted Miguel's back with his hands.

Jennifer laughed. "Mikey's trying to help."

Miguel spun around, holding out his arms. "He's a big help. Can I hold him?"

As she poured Mikey into his arms, Jennifer said, "For a few minutes while I get out his diaper bag."

Miguel bounced his son in his arms. "I'm changing his diaper. I still need lots of practice."

"You don't need to twist my arm." Jennifer spread out the diaper changing pad on the floor and whipped out a new diaper. "It's all yours, Dad."

Miguel changed Mikey's diaper with no help from Jennifer and then tucked the boy against his shoulder. "I think he's tired again."

"He's all confused. I don't think he's ever been awake at two in the morning other than waking up in his crib as a baby."

"Are you confused?" Miguel pressed his lips against Mikey's soft hair and bounced him in the age-old motion for soothing a child. It had come to him naturally.

Jennifer put away the items from the diaper bag, and then collapsed on the bed, crossing her legs at the ankles. "It's a good thing he slept the whole way because he's figured out how to release the straps on his car seat and wriggle out."

Mikey lifted his head from Miguel's shoulder long enough to murmur, "Bad car seat."

Jennifer rolled her eyes. "The car seat is not bad, Mikey. Mommy and even Daddy wear seat belts in the car. Didn't you see Daddy buckle his seat belt?"

Miguel whispered as he gave Mikey another bounce. "I don't think he heard a word you said, Jen. He's drifting off."

"Stubborn, just like his daddy." She yawned and punched the pillows behind her head.

"Get some sleep. I'll put Mikey in the crib when he's ready."

"You're the one who had driving duty. You should sleep and I'll take care of Mikey."

"You've been doing it all for eighteen months." He traced Mikey's ear with his fingertip. "It's my turn."

Jennifer must've sensed the futility of arguing with him or she was too tired to care. She rolled to her side, pulling her knees up to her chest.

Mikey didn't last much longer than his mother. His little body had gone limp against Miguel's chest, and a thin line of drool from his open mouth had made its way to Miguel's shirt.

Miguel crept to the crib and placed Mikey on top of the blanket Jennifer had spread over the hotel's crib sheet. The boy stirred and twitched as Miguel eased his arms from him and pulled another blanket over his son's body.

Miguel watched Mikey for another ten minutes before inching away from the crib. He sat at the window and watched the blinking lights of El Paso in the distance.

He had to try to contact Josh again, or one of his other teammates, to find out if the rumors about him and his time in captivity were gaining ground.

He didn't want or expect to be hailed as a hero when he'd escaped from the enemy, but he hadn't expected his country to turn on him either.

He had to see his family to safety first, and then he'd take care of the rest. Rooting out the mole in the intelligence community would not only restore his own reputation, it would also save lives.

And after the loss of life he'd witnessed when that SEAL team was ambushed, he'd do anything to spare other families that torture.

THE FOLLOWING MORNING, they allowed Mikey to run around the hotel room and bounce on the bed to burn off some energy.

"I don't think we're going to be as lucky today with Mikey. He's a bundle of motion." Jennifer wedged a hand on her hip as she stood next to the bed to make sure Mikey didn't roll off.

"We'll have to see that he has plenty of toys

to keep him occupied, or maybe for lunch we can stop in at one of those fast-food places with a play area." Miguel pulled out his laptop. "I'm going to take advantage of the Wi-Fi in here and try to get a message to Josh, or one of the other guys."

Jennifer zipped up the diaper bag and placed it on top of her suitcase. Then she snatched the car keys from the credenza. "It's pretty hot out there. I'll get Mikey down to the car and start it up to get the AC going."

He nodded as he logged in to his computer and visited the public chat room that he and Josh had designated as their anonymous place to communicate after that last text. He closed out and slipped his laptop into its sleeve, and then lugged all the bags downstairs.

Jennifer was coming around the back of the car and popped open the trunk. She shaded her eyes from the sun with one hand and called out, "I'll start the car to get the air-conditioning going. Are you sure you don't want me to drive this first leg of the trip?"

"Okay. You can drive if you want."

She pushed up the trunk and ducked inside.

One of the suitcases he was dragging behind him twisted to the side, and as he righted it, the motel clerk from the night before raised a coffee cup in his direction. "There's free coffee in the lobby if you want to get a couple of cups for the road."

Miguel looked up. "We just might do that."

Jennifer gave him a thumbs-up from the trunk. "Made some space."

The clerk glanced over her shoulder. "Is your car okay now?"

Miguel cocked his head. "It always was. What do you mean?"

"Oh." She squinted at the car. "Yeah, that's the car. A tow truck was parked next to it early this morning and the driver was beneath the car."

Miguel's heart slammed against his chest as he dropped the suitcase handles and lurched toward the open driver's-side door. "Jennifer! Stop! Don't start the car!"

Her face turned toward him, eyes and mouth open wide as the engine turned over. "I—I..."

"Get out of the car!"

As Jennifer scrambled from the front seat, smoke started curling from the steering column.

Miguel sprang toward her and grabbed her arm, yanking her toward him. He spun her around so he was between her and the car and lunged forward, going airborne and taking her with him.

The explosion from the car propelled them even farther, and Miguel felt a flash of heat at his back.

Jennifer bucked beneath him, coughing and clawing at the ground. "Mikey! Mikey's in the car."

And then Miguel's world went as black as the smoke swirling around them.

Chapter Seven

Her ears were ringing, but she could still hear her own screaming.

Miguel, who'd been covering her body with his own, jumped up and ran back to the burning car.

She struggled to sit up, hacking and trying to spit the acrid taste of burning rubber from her mouth. Tears streamed down her face, stinging her eyes, blurring her vision. But what she saw in front of her made her sick, hollowed out her heart. Nobody inside that car could've survived.

On her hands and knees, the dirt and gravel digging into her flesh, she crawled around to the back of the burning car where she'd last seen Miguel.

The clerk was shouting something behind her, but the words made no sense.

Then Miguel emerged from the billowing smoke, Mikey clutched to his chest.

Jennifer blinked at the vision. It was a dream, a sweet, sweet dream.

"Stay back, Jen. I've got him. I've got our boy."

She collapsed on the ground, laughing and crying at the same time, her tears mingling with the soot and the dirt on her face.

Crouching beside her, Miguel placed a hand on her shoulder. "Can you get up?"

"Yeah." She dragged a hand across her nose, smearing God knew what across her face, and grabbed Miguel's arm.

He pulled her up, and she wrapped her arms around Mikey and Miguel at the same time. The ringing in her ears had subsided and now she could hear Mikey crying, the hotel clerk babbling hysterically behind her and the wail of sirens.

Miguel placed an arm around her and guided her away from the wreckage of her car, still blazing in the parking lot. He led her to the front of the motel and sank to the steps, pulling her down beside him.

She turned to Miguel and brushed her hands across his soot-blackened face. "How did Mikey survive that?"

"He unbuckled the straps on his car seat when you went around to the trunk. You'd left the back door open, thank God, and he squiggled out of the car." Miguel pointed to the wrought iron gate around the small pool. "He wanted to look at the pool. It saved his life."

"Thank God for my negligence in leaving that back door open." She patted Mikey's back. "What was he doing when you found him?"

"The blast had definitely thrown him." He pinched Mikey's chin with his fingers, turning his tear-streaked face toward her. "He has a cut over his eye."

Mikey sniffled, hiccuped and reached out for her. Miguel placed Mikey in her lap as the first responders came squealing into the motel parking lot.

"Let me do the talking."

She rested her chin on Mikey's head. "What happened, Miguel? How'd you know?"

"The motel clerk saved you. She mentioned seeing a tow truck parked next to our car this morning and the driver underneath the chassis."

"I didn't even turn over the engine, just clicked the key one turn."

"It must've been set to explode in the first position, or the guy set it incorrectly."

She dug her nails into his biceps. "How'd they find us?"

"I don't know." He drove the heel of his hand against his forehead. "I'm thinking it must've been that ID I used for Raymond Garcia, but that was just this morning and I paid cash, so the motel just used it to hold the room and didn't even run it."

"They couldn't have followed us. I was awake

long enough last night to know there were no cars with us out of Austin." She covered her mouth with one hand. "Could they have bugged my car?"

"I searched all over the car and even used a detector. You saw me."

"Maybe it was some super-duper kind of tracking device immune to detection." She pointed at the police car that had pulled in behind the fire engine. "We have to tell them something."

"We don't know anything. We're Mr. and Mrs. Raymond Garcia on our way to visit family in Los Angeles." Miguel combed bits of debris from her tangled hair.

"But the car is registered to Jennifer Lynch."

Miguel cast an eye at the smoldering remains of her vehicle. "Somehow, I don't think they're gonna be able to trace the car, and if they do?" He shrugged. "Lynch is your maiden name."

Miguel pushed up from the steps and showed his palm to her as she struggled to rise with Mikey attached to her neck. "You can stay here. That would be completely understandable. In fact, I'm going to send the EMTs over here to check out you two."

She watched through slitted eyes, still burning from the smoke and chemicals of the fire, as Miguel sauntered up to the police officer.

He waved his hand back toward her and Mikey, waved a hand toward their room, the car and the motel clerk, who was talking to another officer. Then he turned to the two EMTs hopping from the ambulance and pointed to her and Mikey on the porch.

As the EMTs approached her, Jennifer stood up and immediately threw out a hand to steady herself against the building, her legs wobbling beneath her.

"Check out my son first. He was near the car when it exploded and the blast threw him."

"Sit back down, Ms....?"

"Garcia. Mrs. Garcia, and this is Mikey." She plopped back down on the step, and the EMT leaned forward and lifted each of her eyelids with his thumb.

"I'm going to put some drops in your eyes."

With the drops swimming in her eyes, Jennifer glanced sideways at the EMT cleaning and bandaging Mikey's cut. "Is he okay? His ears? His eyes?"

"The cut's not too deep, and I'm going to check out the rest of his vitals. He's doing great."

Her EMT had her open wide and peered at the back of her throat. He had her cough while he placed a stethoscope on her back.

"I'm going to clean your hands."

He'd turned her hands over and she raised her eyebrows at her scraped and bloody palms. She hadn't even noticed them, but now felt the sting of the broken skin as the EMT wiped them with a pad, and then swiped them again with some antiseptic.

"Any other aches and pains? How's your breathing?"

She took a deep breath and coughed. "It's fine, although I still taste that smokiness."

"That's not unusual." He packed up his kit. "You and your son are very lucky."

She squinted at Miguel, shrugging and spreading his arms as he talked to the officer. He was doing a bang-up impression of a man who knew nothing.

And maybe that wasn't such a stretch for him. What did they really know except some nefarious group of individuals had them in their crosshairs?

Jennifer accelerated on the stretch of desert highway through New Mexico in their new used car. Miguel had paid cash for it to some guy who'd parked it in a school parking lot that doubled as a used-car lot when class wasn't in session.

She glanced at the dashboard clock and swallowed a lump in her throat.

"Everything okay?" Miguel brushed his knuckles across the denim covering her thigh. "Do you want me to drive?"

"My kids are done with graduation and on to middle school—and I missed it."

"I know, but after what happened at the motel back there, you can see how important it was to get out of Austin."

"Get out of Austin—sounds like a country song."

"Maybe we can write one when this is all over."

She flexed her fingers on the steering wheel. "How'd they find us in El Paso?"

"I don't know, Jen." He dragged his knuckles across his jaw. "Maybe it was your car. Maybe it was the credit card. We can't stop and stay the night anywhere on our way to Palm Springs. It's straight through to Tucson in another four hours or so, where we'll stop for gas and food."

"At least Mikey exhausted himself at that play area where we had breakfast, although that wouldn't have been my first choice of food."

"I craved fast food while I was imprisoned, so I was probably as happy as Mikey."

"I can't believe how close we came to losing him." She massaged the pain that suddenly sliced through her temple.

Miguel turned his head and stared out the window. "My world came to an end for a few minutes until I saw him against that fence. When he turned to look at me, crying and covering his ears, it started up again."

She adjusted the rearview mirror to take in Mikey strapped securely in his new car seat just to make sure he was still there. "That car bomb was intended to take out all of us. They knew we'd all be getting in that car and once you started the engine…"

"These people are ruthless."

"Which people, Miguel? The terrorists who held you captive, or the mole or some other government agency?"

"I'm beginning to think they're one and the same. The mole who infiltrated our intelligence community is working with the terrorists and they're after us now. The mole is not using the government to commit these acts."

"And they want to destroy you…and us. Why?"

"Revenge, or perhaps they think I know too much about the structure of Vlad's organization."

"I hope your brother can help us, or at least keep us safe until you get this information to the right people, the people who can ferret out the mole."

Miguel nodded once and jabbed a button on the radio to start scanning for stations.

She wrinkled her nose at the scratchy reception of a hard rock song. "Too bad we didn't get the model with the CD player or satellite radio."

"Didn't have much time to shop."

"I'm not going to ask you where you got that wad of cash."

"Don't."

They drove for a few more hours of unrelenting desert landscape before Mikey decided he'd had enough of napping.

He piped up from the backseat. "Bad car seat."

Jennifer reached around behind her and squeezed his chubby leg. She whispered to Miguel. "I almost feel like agreeing with him now. If he'd stayed strapped in his car seat…"

Miguel twisted in his seat. "This is a new car seat, Mikey. This is a good car seat. Make sure you leave the straps on, just like Mommy and Daddy do."

Mikey kicked his feet. "Good, good, good. Mikey read."

Miguel picked up the book on the floor of the backseat and flipped it open. "Do you want to read about the moose and the mouse?"

"He's hiding. Mouse is hiding."

Jennifer smiled at Mikey in the rearview mirror. "You know that story, don't you?"

Mikey pointed at Miguel. "He read."

"Daddy. That's your daddy."

"Daddy read."

"You up for it, Daddy?"

"Sure. I don't know this one."

Miguel read the story aloud to Mikey, turning the book toward him to show him the pictures after he finished reading each page.

He was such a hit, Mikey demanded he read it all over again.

Jennifer poked Miguel in the ribs. "I forgot to warn you. This could go on for another three or four readings."

"That's fine. I can handle it. What else do I have to do in the middle of the desert with you at the wheel?"

As she drove, Jennifer listened to the chatter between Miguel and his son and grinned like a crazy person at the natural rapport between the two of them.

Miguel had always wanted children, and he'd made that clear to her from the moment their relationship had started to deepen into something more serious. While he'd teased her about her perfect upbringing, he'd wanted nothing more than to emulate it.

Miguel had always been great with older kids, had mentored teenage boys through his church and helped coach baseball at the high school.

Now he was a father, and it couldn't be under worse circumstances. She put one hand on her stomach to quell the guilt that flared there. Of course, she was just happy to have him home, alive. Life couldn't be all rainbows and unicorns, and Miguel needed to know she'd stand by him no matter what.

She hadn't realized she'd allowed a little sigh to escape her lips until Miguel stopped his game of thumb war with Mikey and asked, "Are you okay? Do you want to take a break from driving?"

"I wouldn't mind a bathroom stop and something to drink. Only two more hours until Tucson. Are you going to want to stop to eat or blow right through after we get gas?"

"Let's stop." He pinched the toe of Mikey's shoe. "I think this guy needs a break from his car seat—his *good* car seat, right, Mikey?"

"Thumb war, Daddy."

"You've created a monster, Miguel."

"Cutest little monster I've ever seen."

Jennifer caught her bottom lip between her teeth. Miguel had seen plenty of monsters.

She wished this car ride could go on forever.

THEY ROLLED INTO Tucson in the early evening when the heat was still shimmering off the pavement and the saguaro cacti raised their arms toward the glorious sunset over the Catalina Foothills.

Miguel had looked up a pizza place before their arrival, and Jennifer pulled the car into the parking lot.

Mikey had been awake almost the entire journey from El Paso, and Jennifer hoped that meant he'd sleep on the six-hour drive to Miguel's brother's place.

When they got out of the car, Miguel stood at attention while she unbuckled Mikey from his car seat. The set of his jaw and his rigid muscles told her he still expected trouble.

"Nobody followed us, Miguel. It's impossible."

His gaze darted around the half-empty parking lot. "They followed us to El Paso."

"It must've been the car. That's gone."

He rolled his shoulders. "Let's get some pizza."

Jennifer ordered a large pizza with everything on it for her and Miguel and a small cheese pizza for Mikey. Miguel made sure they took a seat by the window, where they could keep an eye on the car.

Miguel refilled his soda and slid into the booth across from her. "I'll take over the driving duties. Just have to make sure I'm properly caffeinated."

She waved her pizza crust at his plate, where he'd just dropped his fourth piece of pizza. "Is pizza another craving you had in captivity?" She batted her eyelashes, hoping the flirtatious gesture would prompt him to admit that he'd craved her—because it sure didn't seem as if he had.

Even when they'd touched and kissed, he'd seemed reserved, and they hadn't made love yet. Granted, the conditions hadn't been optimal the two nights they'd been together, but in the old days they would've found a way to be together. The old days—before his capture…and torture.

"Yeah, pizza, beer and a baseball game on TV."

She slumped against the booth's bolster and

stuffed the crust in her mouth. So much for her flirting skills.

"Balls, Mommy. Play with the balls?"

"I was hoping he wouldn't see that ball pool." Jennifer wiped her hands on a napkin and crumpled it beside her plate. "Do we have time to hit the ball pool?"

"Sure. He'll sleep all the way to Palm Springs for sure." Miguel's gaze darted among the patrons of the pizza parlor for the hundredth time. He'd been watching their comings and goings ever since they took a seat.

"We won't be long." She plucked Mikey from the restaurant's high chair and carried him toward the small ball pool on the far side of the game room around the corner from the dining room.

She yanked aside the netting that enclosed the circular play area and lowered Mikey onto the surface of the plastic balls undulating like a multicolored ocean.

He dived in headfirst and grabbed a ball in each hand. Giggling he rolled onto his back and threw both of the balls at her.

"Oh, you wanna play rough, huh?" She launched off the side of the enclosure, landing next to Mikey and causing him to bob up and down on top of the balls, his arms and legs spread out like a skydiver.

Jennifer scooped up handfuls of balls as she

shimmied past Mikey toward the other side of the ball pool.

She twisted her head over her shoulder to see if Mikey was following her and gasped as a man slid into the ball pool—alone.

Her gaze traveled past his shoulder looking for an accompanying child. Then she saw a glint of metal in his hand, and she knew he wasn't here to play.

Chapter Eight

The man brandished the knife in front of him.

Jennifer screamed and lunged for Mikey amid all the clacking plastic.

The cacophony of the play room with its clanging levers, beepers and buzzers drowned out her scream. She tried again, this time bellowing Miguel's name.

As the menacing figure waded toward her son, Jennifer grabbed Mikey's ankle and dragged him toward her. She shoveled the plastic orbs on top of his body to bury him in the pool.

Then she started firing plastic balls at the man's head. Plastic might not be much of a match against the cold hard steel of a blade, but it was all she had.

The netting behind the man whipped back and Miguel launched himself at the attacker. They both went down, sinking into the ball pool.

Jennifer held her breath as the plastic balls flew every which way.

Then Miguel popped up. "Hand me Mikey and let's get out. Now."

"Is he...?"

"Now."

She hoisted Mikey beneath the arms and leaned forward, thrusting him at Miguel, who grabbed him and spun around toward the gaping flap of the netting. Jennifer scrambled out of the ball pool, passing by the man now facedown and halfway buried beneath plastic.

Two kids, about the same age as Jennifer's students at school, stood poised at the entrance, their mouths wide-open.

Miguel planted himself in front of them, blocking their view of the ball pool. "Don't go in there. A man's hurt. Tell the guy at the counter."

With Mikey tucked under his arm, Miguel strode to the table Jennifer and Mikey had left barely ten minutes ago and gathered up everything, including her purse.

Soon they were outside and Miguel threw open the back door. "Hurry. Get him strapped in, Jen."

"Ball pool. Ball pool," Mikey chanted as Jennifer buckled him into his car seat.

They were on the road two minutes later.

She closed her eyes and took several deep breaths. "What happened to him?"

Miguel glanced at Mikey in the rearview mirror, singing to himself about ball pools.

Twisting around in her seat, Jennifer handed Mikey a yellow ball that she'd inexplicably carried out of the pizza parlor. "Here you go."

Miguel studied Mikey in the mirror for a minute more and then turned up the radio a bit, leaning to the side. "He fell on his knife when I jumped him. I don't know his condition. I didn't want to stick around to find out."

"How did they find us? Again." She crossed her hands over her chest and her heart hammered against her right palm.

"I don't know. They came into the restaurant after we did."

"They?"

"It was that man and a woman. I watched them walk in. They ordered, sat down, ate. Nothing unusual. Then the woman left and it looked like the guy was heading toward the bathrooms, but I watched him and saw him veer off toward the play area. He had no reason to be in there—other than to follow you and Mikey."

"My God. It's a good thing you were watching him. I don't think anyone would've heard us in there."

Miguel pounded a fist on the steering wheel. "How did they know? It can't be this car. We've never even been out of it since we bought it this morning."

"Phones?"

He nodded at the one on the console. "Can't be this one. It's a temp phone I bought in Austin—has never been out of my sight."

"Could it be mine?" She pulled her cell phone from her purse and held it away from her face as if it could detonate in her hand at any minute. "They did break into my place."

"But your phone wasn't there when they did, neither was your laptop."

"Can't be the ID anymore, if that's even what it was before. There is no Raymond Garcia."

"We can't go to my brother's until I figure this out. It won't be a safe house if we lead them right to it. I don't want to put Roberto's security to the test." With his warm hand, he covered her fist, clenched in her lap. "Let's analyze you, first."

She straightened up in her seat. "You checked my car for a device before we left and if they had tracked my car to that motel in El Paso, that device blew up with the car. Like you said, my phone wasn't in my house when they broke in and it hasn't been out of my sight, same with my laptop."

"We're going to pull over in about an hour into a rest area that's halfway to Phoenix. I'm going to go through our luggage. Maybe they put a GPS in your bag, figuring you'd be taking off."

"That's a huge assumption on their part. Beyond a car, phone or laptop, I can't imagine how they'd know what I'd take on the run or even if I'd go on the run. The only thing they could be sure of is me." She jabbed her chest with her thumb. "And I'm pretty sure I didn't swallow a GPS lately."

Miguel made a strange noise in the back of his throat and she glanced at his profile, hard and tense.

"What is it?"

He shifted in his seat and flexed his fingers. "I just got a crazy idea in my head."

"What?"

"I don't know." He lifted his shoulders.

"Don't start keeping things from me now, Miguel."

"Maybe you didn't swallow a GPS, but maybe I did."

JENNIFER JERKED BACK from him, her eyebrows jumping to her hairline. "What are you talking about? How could you swallow a GPS? I was kidding."

"I know you were kidding, but it brought an idea into focus for me that had been wandering around my brain ever since my escape from the debriefing center." He rubbed his jaw and glanced at his sleeping son. Jennifer might think he was deranged, but she'd wanted to hear it all—no craziness spared.

"It brought into focus the idea that you'd swallowed a GPS?" Her hand rested on the passenger door, as if jumping out of a moving car might be an option for her.

"Not swallowed, Jen, had one implanted."

Her already pale face got whiter. "You think a GPS was implanted in your body at the debriefing center?"

"They could've done it without my knowledge." He chewed on his bottom lip for a few seconds. "I was…pretty beat up by the time I got to Maryland. The doctors I first saw in Germany after my escape from captivity didn't do much to treat my injuries—just the basics. The folks in Maryland wanted to get their hands on me."

"Did they treat you in Maryland or just stand around and observe you like some specimen?" Red fury whipped into her cheeks as she dug her fingers into the seat.

"They treated me. Set some bones, stitched me up, gave me meds…lots of meds. I didn't want them but was pretty helpless to stop the doctors. They told me it was for my pain." He snorted and laughed at the same time. "I told them I was impervious to pain after what I'd been through."

Jennifer sucked in a sharp breath and placed a hand on his thigh. "So during this…treatment, you think they could've injected a GPS into your body?"

"Yep. How else is someone tracking our every move?"

"I didn't even know that could be done."

"You've owned dogs. Didn't you ever have them microchipped?"

"That's a dog. You're a man." She smacked her hands against the dashboard, her anger on his behalf practically steaming from her ears.

"Shh, you'll wake Mikey." Miguel put his finger to his lips. "It's actually a little different, since the pet microchips don't use GPS technology—but there is a GPS chip, as well. The CIA has used them before."

"What would make you think they used one on you? How would you even know where they put it?"

"Oh, I have a good idea." He rolled his body to the side a little and smacked his hand against his right hip. "I had a lot of lacerations in that area and the docs spent time suturing there. It was sore, always felt sore those first few days. My flesh felt bumpy. Even now there's some irritation."

"You mentioned your sore hip before." Jennifer pressed her hand against the window. "So they might be following us on some computer screen somewhere right now."

"They probably are, but we're going to put a stop to it tonight."

"How?" She whipped her head around so fast, strands of her blond hair got stuck to her lipstick.

"We're gonna get to that rest stop first and see if my hunch is correct. Then we'll deal with it."

Hitching up her shoulders, she crossed her arms and stayed that way for the next half hour. When the headlights of the car picked out the sign at the side of the road announcing a rest stop, Jennifer tapped the window. "Here we go."

Miguel signaled and exited the road, pulling into a parking space at the rest area. With the car at a standstill, Mikey dug his fists into his eyes and made mewling noises.

"I knew he'd wake up once the car stopped." Jennifer rubbed Mikey's chubby leg.

"That's all right. Let him stretch his legs and maybe he'll be ready to sleep the rest of the way to Palm Springs."

"If we go to Palm Springs."

"We'll be there." Miguel shoved open his door. "I'm going in the bathroom to check things out. Why don't you take Mikey to the ladies' room so you're close by?"

Jennifer gave him a stiff nod.

He waited while she got Mikey out of the car and hooked the diaper bag over her shoulder. As they approached the bathrooms, Jennifer tugged on his sleeve. "Even better. We'll go into the family restroom."

Miguel glanced at the sign on the door of mommy, daddy and kid stick figures. "Perfect. Never paid much attention to these bathrooms before."

"I'm not sure the proponents of family bathrooms ever imagined a family like us."

"Takes all kinds." Miguel shoved open the door for Jennifer and Mikey and then locked it behind them.

He pulled his tracking device from his pocket. "This should pick up some waves."

"From your body?"

"That's what I'm hoping." He unzipped his fly and yanked down his jeans over his right hip. "You're going to have to do it, Jen. I can't see. It'll make the needle waver."

He ran his fingers over his flesh, still rough from its former treatment, prodding the sore spot that he'd had ever since he left Maryland. "Try right here, but wave the tracker over your hand first as a control."

"Can you hold Mikey? I don't want to put him on this bathroom floor, even though it looks pretty clean."

"Sure." He turned and scooped his son into his arms. "You ready for some activity, big boy?"

"Ball pool?"

"No ball pool here," Miguel murmured under his breath. "Thank God."

Jennifer was breathing heavily behind him and he felt her warm breath on the top of his bare buttocks.

"Well?"

"Not only is the needle on the detector bouncing—" she pressed her cool fingers against his skin "—I can actually see an outline of something beneath your flesh, Miguel."

"That's it then. They've been tracking *me*."

"That's so wrong. It's creepy. Very *1984*-ish."

"I feel better that we found the answer—and now we can deal with it."

"How? How are we going to deal with this? How are you going to waltz into some doctor's office and ask him—or her—to remove a GPS from your ass?"

"That far down, huh?"

"I never thought I'd be the one telling you this, Miguel, but be serious. What are we going to do?"

"Not we—you."

"Me?" She stepped around to face him, as he pretended to grab Mikey's nose between his fingers.

With his other hand, he dug into his pocket and pulled out a switchblade. "With this."

"No." She stumbled back. "I can't do that. We have nothing here."

"We have this." He waved the knife at her. "And some soap, water and paper towels. We even have some clean cloths in the diaper bag."

"Miguel, I'm a teacher, not a surgeon."

"You don't need to be a surgeon to dig a little

metal device out of someone's backside—especially mine."

"What does that mean?"

"Didn't I tell you? I'm impervious to pain. Wash the area with soap and water, or use one of those diaper wipes, pat it dry and dig in."

"I can't."

He turned with Mikey in his arms and gripped one of her shoulders. "I've never heard you say that before, Jen, and now isn't the time to start. If you can't get this out of me, I'll send you and Mikey to my brother's by yourselves and I'll find some other way to get rid of this GPS—even if I have to do it myself."

Her Adam's apple bobbed in her slender throat. "Okay. I'll do it."

"That's my fearless girl. I'll hang onto Mikey."

A knock on the bathroom door made them both freeze, but neither of them answered.

Jennifer zipped open the diaper bag and plucked several wipes from the plastic container.

Miguel flinched as the cold, wet wipe touched his skin. "Poor Mikey. That's cold. You should warm those things up before you wipe his bottom."

She crumpled the wipes and tossed them into the trash can. She probed the area with her fingertips and let out a heavy breath.

He blinked once as the knife gouged his flesh. Then he gritted his teeth and made funny faces at Mikey, who finally stopped squirming in his arms.

"Are you getting it?"

"I'm afraid of hurting you."

"Piece of cake. Get the edge of the knife beneath the device and lift it."

"I almost…"

She released a little sob as a sharp pain shivered down his leg from his buttocks.

"I have it. I just need to maneuver it out. You're bleeding, Miguel."

"I'd expect that. Won't be the first blood I've shed. Won't be the last. Keep going."

Another minute and Jennifer cried out, "I have it."

"Keep it on the edge of the knife, clean me up and start applying some pressure."

She held the bloody knife over his right shoulder. "Do you want to take it?"

Shifting Mikey on his left hip, he took the handle of the knife, a small, gray oblong object on the tip. "Little bastard."

"I've cleaned it as much as I can with the wipes." She pressed a soft cloth to the wound. "Can you get your jeans over this and then hold it in place until we get to the car? I'll drive."

"I feel a hundred pounds lighter. Take Mikey." After Jen took Mikey from his arms, Miguel placed the knife on the edge of the sink. He wrapped up the bloody wipes in some paper towels and dropped them into the trash. Spying some drops of blood on the floor, Miguel wiped those up. Then he washed his hands and rinsed off the device that had been implanted in his body in Maryland on God-knows-whose orders.

After cleaning the knife, he pocketed it. "We're good to go. Mikey okay?"

"He's fine. You entertained him so much, he didn't notice a thing. Are you okay?"

"I'm good." The wound throbbed but he'd felt worse—much worse.

He unlocked the door and a woman carrying a toddler about Mikey's age sprang up from the bench. "You wouldn't happen to have a diaper I can borrow, would you? We'll stop in Phoenix to buy more, but I'm fresh out and my daughter is in desperate need."

"Of course." Jennifer reached into the diaper bag and pulled out a fresh diaper. "Here you go and sorry we took so long in there."

"Oh, I know how it is. Thank you so much."

"Where are you headed?" Miguel took the diaper bag from Jennifer.

"We're going to swing through Phoenix, and then we're going to San Diego for my cousin's wedding."

Miguel pulled a diaper from the bag and tucked it into the diaper bag hanging over the woman's shoulder. "Take an extra—just in case."

"Thank you. I appreciate it and so does

Chloe." She bounced her daughter in her arms before turning toward the family bathroom.

Miguel got to the car and peeled his jeans from his hip. The blood hadn't seeped through the cloth yet. He applied more pressure as he watched Jennifer chase Mikey around in a circle.

She lured him back into the car by buying him an ice-cream bar from the vending machine. Once Mikey was in his car seat, Jennifer gave him a few more licks of the vanilla ice cream beneath the chocolate shell.

"Daddy's turn." She handed the ice-cream bar to Miguel. "You can finish that off. You've been such a good patient."

She started the car and pulled out of the rest stop, heading toward Phoenix as the darkness washed over the desert landscape. "Did you throw that GPS in the trash at the rest stop?"

"What would be the fun in that?"

She raised her eyebrows without turning her head. "Fun?"

"That GPS is headed to a wedding in San Diego."

Chapter Nine

The throbbing in his hip kept Miguel awake as Jennifer drove through the night.

After the excitement in the ball pool and a dash around the rest stop, Mikey slept the sleep of the innocent, tucked away in his car seat. Miguel twisted around and drank in his son's sweet face for the hundredth time. He'd never get tired of looking at him, marveling at his perfect nails on the tips of his perfect fingers and the way his ear curved into a soft semicircle.

"He's pretty amazing, isn't he?" Jennifer tipped her head toward the backseat.

"You're pretty amazing." He pinched her knee. "He's a happy, healthy boy and you did that all by yourself."

"I did have some help. You should've heard some of those early conversations with my mom." She rolled her eyes. "You never would've guessed that I'd read about a hundred books on taking care of a baby."

"They worked. Mikey's doing great, looks great."

"You haven't seen a total toddler meltdown yet. You might change your mind after that spectacle."

"I doubt it." He yawned. "We crossed into California. Not much longer."

"Are you going to call your brother and let him know we're on the way? It's going to be past midnight when we get there."

"I'm not going to give him any advance notice. I think it's safer this way. It'll also give me a look at how robust his security is."

"As long as he doesn't shoot us on sight." Jennifer sent him a sidelong glance. "How are you feeling?"

"The wound is sore, but nothing that won't heal."

"You still need to see a doctor."

"That'll be a hard one to explain." He reached back and pressed the cloth against the area and then held up his fingers. "No blood. It hasn't seeped through at all."

"Maybe not, but the wound was pretty deep. I oughta know. I'm the one who gouged you."

"And I'm grateful for it."

She bit her bottom lip. "You don't think that

couple with the little girl will be in trouble, do you?"

"No. They'll be tracked to San Diego. The people after us will be watching wherever it is they land, and they won't see us there. They'll probably figure out what we did."

"What's going on, Miguel? People, doctors at the debriefing center in Maryland, implanted a GPS tracking device in your body and now they're trying to kill you?" She glanced in her rearview mirror. "Kill Mikey?"

"The doctors may not have known why they were doing what they were doing. They could've been told…something."

"Something what?" Her knuckles turned white as she gripped the steering wheel.

"They could've been told I was dangerous. That I was unhinged by my captivity and the navy had to keep an eye on me."

"That might explain why they went along with the tracking device, but what about the people at the center?"

"Most of them probably don't know what's going on. This whole—" he waved one hand in the air "—operation could be the work of one or two people, one or two bad apples on the task force."

"Bad apples?" She swore, which he noticed she never did around Mikey. "I think they go be-yond bad apples. Bad apples skim a little money off the top. They don't murder people and their families…children."

"Rotten apples, then."

"Do these rotten apples know about your brother? They must. I know you had to go through a security background. Someone in your past like Roberto is bound to raise red flags."

"They probably do, although Roberto is now officially Rob Eastwood. He might be hard to connect to me. It's also in my file that I had very little contact with my brother. But these rogue agents, these moles, are not going to get very far with Roberto."

"I hope you're right."

Another hour of driving brought them to Palm Springs, and Miguel gave her directions toward the foothills of the San Jacinto Mountains and Roberto's compound. The car turned on an unmarked and unlit desert road, and Jennifer flicked on the brights.

"Are you sure it's out here?" She hunched over the steering wheel and peered at the patch of road illuminated by the headlights.

"Positive. Even though I've never been here, I memorized the location and Roberto's directions."

The car hit a bump, and all at once, a bright white light flooded the entire area. A high sandy-colored wall rose before them, and Jen slammed on the brakes.

"Whoa! Where did that come from?"

Miguel scooted forward in his seat and tipped back his head, taking in two armed guards on the wall. "Where did they come from?"

"Oh, my God. I told you they'd shoot us on sight."

"Stay in the car." Miguel slid outside and the cool mountain air lifted the ends of his hair. He held his hands over his head, and the speaker to his left crackled to life.

"Who are you and what do you want?"

"I'm Miguel Estrada. Roberto is my brother."

The disembodied voice continued, "Take two steps to your right."

Miguel complied, his hands still raised. He tilted his head back, staring straight into the camera that had tracked his movement.

Several seconds passed and the speaker crackled again. "Who's in the car with you?"

"My fiancée and our son."

"Have them get out of the car."

Miguel turned back toward the car and gestured to Jennifer.

She stumbled from the car. "Th-they still have guns on us."

"Get Mikey out of the car and join me beneath the camera."

"Is this any kind of family welcome?"

"It's why we're here."

She ducked into the car and emerged with Mikey in her arms, blinking in the bright lights.

Miguel pulled her next to him, and they faced the camera together. Another few seconds passed and the voice directed them to the right of the compound.

More lights turned on and a heavy gate rolled open. Jennifer started forward, but Miguel grabbed her arm. "Wait."

The instructions continued, "The woman and child first."

"Go on." Miguel nudged Jennifer and she shuffled forward.

His gut lurched when he saw a man come out of the shadows to wave a wand over Jen and Mikey. At least they hadn't asked her to hand over Mikey. That would've been a problem.

They were ushered beyond his view, and a shot of adrenaline coursed through Miguel's system.

"Now you, with your hands out to your sides."

As he walked through the gate, Miguel called out, "I have a gun and a knife in the car, but nothing on me."

The same guy who had waved the wand over Jennifer stepped forward and subjected Miguel to the same treatment. Then he got an additional pat-down.

He winced as the heavy hand hit his hip.

The man growled. "What's that?"

"A fresh wound."

"Lemme see."

This felt like a strip search but Miguel kept his mouth shut. He didn't want to give this goon any ideas.

Miguel unzipped his fly and tugged down his jeans on his right side, over the white cloth Jen had first applied in the bathroom outside of Phoenix.

The security guard called over someone else. "C'mon over here and take a look at this. He claims it's a fresh wound."

Another man came forward, tucking a weapon in the back of his waistband. He crouched forward and peeled off the makeshift bandage.

Miguel grunted as the cloth separated from the dried blood and gouged flesh.

"What the hell happened here? That's not a bullet wound."

"It's a knife wound."

Jennifer came charging back toward the main gate, one of the security personnel in helpless pursuit. She descended on them like an avenging angel, the compound's search lights highlighting her blond hair and creating a glow around her head.

"You idiots! You made it bleed again after we'd stanched it."

"*Idiots* is an apt description. That's my little

brother. He's a goddamn war hero. Leave him the hell alone."

"Roberto?" Miguel hiked up his jeans and pushed past the security guards, grabbing Jennifer's hand.

His brother enveloped him, Jen and Mikey in a bear hug. "Sorry about the security, Miguel. When I saw you on camera, I told them to let you through—no questions asked."

"Not a problem."

Jennifer squirmed away from the group hug. "Actually, there is a problem. Miguel has an injury on his hip and your overzealous security team ripped off his bandage and now it's bleeding."

Miguel curled an arm around Jennifer's waist. "Roberto, this is Jennifer, my fiancée, and this big guy is my son."

"I saw him on the security camera. No mistaking he's yours." Roberto took Jennifer's hand. "Nice to meet you, Jennifer, and don't worry about Miguel. I have a doctor on call, and I'll get him out here as soon as possible."

"Thank you." Jennifer clasped Roberto's hand in both of hers.

"What are we standing out here for? Let's get inside. Are you hungry, thirsty, need a drink?"

Miguel took Mikey from Jennifer's arms. "All of the above."

Roberto led them to a golf cart. "The house is tucked back from the road and the front gate."

Miguel handed Jennifer into the front seat next to his brother, while he swung up on the back. He settled Mikey in his lap, and the cart lurched forward and crawled up the drive with three armed security guards following it on foot.

Yeah, they'd come to the right place.

His brother's palatial home rose from the desert floor like some spaceship that had lost its way and then switched on some camouflage magic when it crash-landed.

The muted lights indicated a house asleep, but Roberto was full of energy. He hopped out of the golf cart. "I apologize that I'm the only one to greet you. My wife and children are sleeping."

Jennifer took Roberto's hand as he helped her out of the cart. "We're the ones who should apologize for arriving so late and unannounced."

"My little brother is welcome here anytime. He always was."

Miguel slipped off the back of the cart and set Mikey on the ground, holding his hand. "He wants to walk."

"Of course he does." Roberto slapped Miguel on the back. "He's probably been cooped up in the car for…miles."

"I'll tell you the whole story, Rob, but Jen needs to sit down and have a shot of something. It's been a rough night."

Jennifer corrected him, "Rough couple of nights—and days."

As they ascended the broad steps to the double doors into the house, a housekeeper appeared in the doorway.

Roberto nodded once and asked her in Spanish to call Dr. Paz, have two rooms made up and to get some cookies and milk for Mikey. She melted away before they even crossed the threshold.

"This way to the great room." Roberto winked. "There's a wet bar in there."

"I don't want to bleed on your expensive sofa." Miguel released Mikey's hand and his boy made a beeline to the corner of the room where a train set gleamed and beckoned.

"I'll get you a towel from behind the bar."

Jennifer took off after Mikey. "Shh, Mikey. Don't make a lot of noise. People are sleeping."

"Jennifer, please sit." Roberto crouched beside the train set and flicked a switch, bringing the cars to life. "My wife, Gabriela, and the children have rooms in the back of the house on the third floor. They're not going to hear a thing."

When Jen collapsed on one end of the sofa and closed her eyes, a knife twisted in Miguel's gut. She'd been through the ringer and hadn't complained once, had kept it all together. Now she needed a minute or two to fall apart.

Roberto shoved a clean bar towel against Miguel's chest. "Try this."

Miguel loosened his jeans and peeled the bloody cloth from his backside and pressed the fresh one against the wound.

Roberto returned with a tray of three shot glasses filled to the brim with a light golden liquid, a sliced lime, a dish of salt and a bottle of tequila.

Jennifer opened one eye. "You're kidding."

"It'll do you good." Roberto handed a shot glass to Miguel.

"It'll do me in."

"That, too." Miguel picked up a slice of lime with two fingers, squeezed it slightly, touched it to the salt, sucked it between his teeth and clinked his glass with his brother's.

That first blast of tequila down his throat hummed through his blood and loosened his muscles. Here at his brother's place with others to watch over Jen and Mikey, Miguel could let go a little.

After a few more shots, Jennifer curled up in her corner of the sofa, resting her head on the padded arm. "I'm done."

Miguel massaged the arch of her bare foot. "You and your son both."

He pointed to Mikey curled up like his mom, next to the train track, fast asleep.

"We should get him to bed." Jen closed her eyes and didn't make a move.

"He's fine where he is and so are you."

Roberto wedged one expensive loafer on the coffee table. "So, what brings you here, Miguel? You swore you'd never step foot in any home of mine."

"You've gone legit, haven't you? More or less?"

"More or less. I work for some big names, people you'd recognize, fixing their lives."

"Must be dangerous. You live in a fortress. You changed your name."

His brother narrowed his eyes. "That's why you're here, isn't it?"

Miguel studied his older brother's dark eyes and tossed off the rest of the tequila in his shot glass. "I'm in trouble, Rob."

"I figured you'd have to be to come out here to see me." Roberto raised both hands when Miguel opened his mouth. "Is it something I can fix for you?"

"No, it's not like that."

"I also figured it wouldn't be anything like what my clients get mixed up with—drugs, rape, hookers."

This time Miguel stopped his brother. "I don't need to hear anything else about what you do. It's nothing like that. It's not for myself. I need you to take care of Jennifer and Mikey while I handle some business."

"Of course." Roberto brushed salt from his

fingertips into the plate. "What business is it? Military business?"

"Something like that. I was captured by the enemy two years ago, and now I don't know who that enemy is anymore."

While Miguel launched into the details of his escape and transport to the hospital in Germany first and then the debriefing center in Maryland, Roberto steepled his fingers and asked measured questions. Miguel got a good picture of why his brother's clients trusted him with their lives and fortunes.

As Miguel came to the end of his story, one of Roberto's security guards hovered at the entrance to the great room and cleared his throat.

"Excuse me, sir. Dr. Paz has arrived."

Miguel rose from the sofa and stretched. "Before he starts working on me, I'm going to get Jennifer and Mikey into a real bed." He nudged Jennifer's shoulder. "Jen. Wake up."

Her lids flew open and she bolted upright. "Is it Mikey?"

"He's fine." Miguel squeezed one of her shoulders. "He's still sleeping on the floor. The doctor's here. You and Mikey can follow Patricia, our housekeeper, up to your rooms."

Jennifer uncurled her legs and crept toward their son's sleeping form. She crouched beside him and gathered him in her arms.

Miguel swept Mikey's hair from his forehead and whispered, "Do you need help?"

"No. I'll get him down. You just do everything the doctor says."

"Will do. I'll be up later."

When Dr. Paz arrived, they moved into the kitchen and Miguel showed him the wound. "I had...something implanted under my skin and my fiancée had to dig it out with a knife."

"She didn't do a bad job, considering." The doctor pushed his glasses to the end of his nose.

Jennifer's voice rose above their murmurs. "I sterilized the knife and the area with just a baby wipe, so I'm worried about infection."

All three men turned their heads to look at Jen as she marched into the kitchen.

"I thought you'd gone up to bed." Miguel sucked in a breath when the doctor pressed a wet, soapy cloth to the wound.

"I said I'd get Mikey settled. If you thought I was going to drift off to dreamland while you were down here getting poked and prodded, you don't know me very well."

"Nothing you can do down here, Jen."

Roberto crossed his arms and snorted. "She can make sure you follow the doctor's orders."

"Your big brother has more sense than you do."

"I like this woman, Miguel." Roberto kicked out a stool. "Have a seat, Jennifer."

Dr. Paz peppered Jennifer with questions as he cleaned and sterilized the site.

"I'm going to have to give you a few stitches, but you'll be as good as new with probably just a small scar."

"One of many." Miguel shrugged.

The doctor held out two small bottles, one in each hand, and shook them. "Antibiotics and painkillers. Take one of each. The painkillers are also anti-inflammatories, so don't try to tough it out. Two a day for the antibiotics until the bottle is gone and probably one full day of painkillers unless you need more."

"Thank you, Dr. Paz." Roberto clapped him on the back. "Thanks for coming out at this time."

Dr. Paz peeled off his gloves and repacked his bag. "Day, night—time is meaningless when it comes to your clients, Rob."

"Miguel is much more than a client."

"Then he came to the right place." Dr. Paz shook hands all around, and a security guard walked him outside.

"You two try to get some sleep, and we'll discuss a plan tomorrow. Sleep in as long as you like. The kids' nanny can take care of Mikey if he wakes up early. He can meet his cousins."

Under Jennifer's watchful gaze, Miguel popped two pills into his mouth and downed them with a glass of water. "I suppose I should've told the doc that I'd had several shots of tequila."

"I think he could tell. The combination with the painkillers will probably just put you to sleep sooner, and from what I can tell, you need the rest." Roberto waved off the security guards hanging around the door. "Secure the perimeter of the compound. Make sure nobody followed my brother or the doctor."

Patricia materialized at the foot of the staircase. "I'll show you to your room. Your little one is sound asleep."

Their bags waited for them in the corner of a room adjoining Mikey's on the second floor of the house.

Jennifer pointed to another door. "That's the bathroom. It's already stocked with soaps and shampoos and big, fluffy towels. I'm going to get ready for bed, unless you want the bathroom first."

"Go ahead. I'm going to get these jeans off."

Jennifer disappeared into the bathroom, and Miguel yanked off his jeans, which now sported a round spot of blood.

After sitting on the edge of the bed to remove his pants, Miguel couldn't muster the energy to stand up. The room spun in a hazy mixture of tequila and pills.

He fell back against the pillows and swung his legs onto the bed. As his heavy lids fell over his eyes, he relaxed every muscle in his body for the first time in days.

And he had one more excuse for not making love to Jennifer.

Chapter Ten

The next morning, Jennifer rolled to her side and burrowed into the pillow, inhaling its fresh scent, as if it had been hung out to dry in a sunshiny breeze. She never hung laundry out on a clothesline.

But she wasn't home. She opened one eye and took in the large, impersonal room.

Shifting onto her back, she flung out one arm into the empty space beside her. Miguel had already vacated the bed.

Disappointment soaked into her bones. She'd hoped his lethargy from the night before would've carried over to the morning, and she'd find him here next to her still asleep. She could've found a few ways to wake him.

She stretched and curled her toes like a cat, but she felt none of the cat's satisfaction after a long sleep.

Squeezing her eyes shut, she tried to concentrate on the positives. They were safe and secure. They'd discovered how they were being followed, and Miguel had seen a doctor who'd patched him up properly.

She shouldn't be whining about not waking up beside her fiancé. He had bigger concerns right now than making love to her.

A tear seeped out of the corner of her eye and she swiped at the trail it left to her ear.

The door of the bedroom edged open.

"Shh. She might be sleeping." Miguel's whisper carried across the room.

Then the door burst wide and Mikey scampered across the floor and flung himself against the side of the bed. "Mommy, help."

She reached over and pulled Mikey onto the bed and into her arms. "Good morning, you little ray of sunshine."

Raising her eyebrows at Miguel still hovering in the doorway, she said, "You're up early after the night we had."

"Not really." He strode into the room and flicked aside the heavy drapes.

Sun spilled into the room, and Jennifer blinked. "What time is it?"

"It's close to ten. Mikey and I slept in until about eight, and then went downstairs for breakfast and a little family reunion."

"Did you meet your cousins, Mikey?" Jennifer grabbed his feet and tipped him back so that he leaned against her raised knees.

"Bobby, Mila and the baby."

She held up three fingers. "You have three cousins? What's the baby's name?"

"He's a baby." Mikey bicycled his legs.

"I know that, but what's his name?"

Miguel sat on the edge of the bed. "I guess the baby is too insignificant to notice. His name is Joey, Joseph. How are you feeling?"

"Me? I'm just fine. You're the one with the knife wound on your hip. The one who collapsed in this bed last night like the dead."

"Yeah, that painkiller on top of the tequila did me in, but I felt great this morning."

She yawned. She supposed they were just going to ignore the fact that they'd had an opportunity to be intimate this morning, and Miguel had passed. She could ignore it but not for much longer.

"What's for breakfast?"

"Pancakes!" Mikey shouted the word.

"My favorite. I'm starving."

Miguel held out his arms. "Mommy's going to get dressed. Do you want to come with me?"

"Pool. Swimming."

"The kids are going in the pool later. Mikey seems excited about it. Has he been in a pool yet?"

"He's had some mommy and me classes at the Y."

"We might all want to hit the pool. I think it's going to be in the nineties today and it's heating up already."

"Bobby?" Mikey rolled off her stomach and crawled toward Miguel. "I see Bobby."

"I think Bobby's going to show you his remote-control cars."

Mikey bounced on the bed until Miguel swept him up. He met Jennifer's gaze over their son's head. "I'll meet you down in the kitchen and keep you company while you eat breakfast."

At least he wanted to keep her company somewhere.

Forty-five minutes later, Jennifer made her way down two flights of stairs to the great room, following the scent of coffee. Standing at the bottom of the staircase, she looked both ways. She couldn't remember the direction of the kitchen from last night.

Patricia turned the corner of the great room and stopped abruptly. "Are you looking for breakfast, missus?"

At least someone thought she was a missus. "Yes, I am."

"Follow me."

Jennifer followed Patricia's long, swinging braid into the informal kitchen, the same kitchen where Dr. Paz had patched Miguel last night. Instead of a doctor's bag, one place setting occupied an area of the butcher-block table.

"I'm the last holdout?"

Patricia cocked her head and her braid swung over her shoulder. "Pardon?"

"I'm the last one to eat breakfast?"

"Yes, but don't worry. We have everything." She clapped her hands twice, and another housekeeper scurried into the breakfast room. Patricia spoke Spanish to the new arrival, much too quickly for Jennifer to catch anything other than *café*.

Jennifer sat at the table and turned her coffee cup over, just like in a restaurant. "*Café, por favor con leche.*"

The second housekeeper nodded as she tried to flatten a smile from her lips.

Jennifer narrowed her eyes. "My Spanish accent is that bad, huh?"

"No, not at all. Very good, missus."

"Call me Jennifer, please."

Once they'd figured out what to call each other, Gracie retreated to the kitchen and reappeared with a steaming coffeepot and a creamer filled to the brim.

"Would you like pancakes, Jennifer? If not, the chef can make you anything."

"Pancakes are fine."

"Blueberry? Banana nut?"

"Oh, for goodness sake. Whatever he has that's easy. Tell him to surprise me."

About ten minutes later, Gracie returned with

a stack of blueberry pancakes, several crisp strips of bacon and a pitcher of what looked like freshly squeezed orange juice. After she delivered the food, Gracie put one hand over her heart and said, "Your little boy? *Qué lindo.*"

"Thank you. I hope he won't be too much trouble."

Her eyes widened and she shook her head before she tripped back to the kitchen, and it occurred to Jennifer that perhaps Roberto didn't keep his household staff apprised of his business or his guests' comings and goings.

She sighed and sawed into her stack of pancakes.

"You going to eat all of that?" Miguel pulled out the chair next to her and snatched a piece of bacon from the serving plate.

"Probably not. Help yourself. You're still not back to your former weight, are you?"

"No." He curled his left biceps. "But I'm working on it."

She averted her gaze from his bulging muscle. Was she supposed to look but not touch? "What's the plan, Miguel? What the heck are the three of us going to do in Palm Springs under lock and key? And at what point will you deem it safe for us to return to our normal lives?"

A shriek and the drumming of little feet nearby brought a smile to Miguel's face. "That's what Mikey's going to do—get to know his cousins and play with all their toys. The kids also have a tutor who works with them through the summer. Mikey doesn't have to miss his preschool, so he won't get behind."

Jennifer flicked her fingers. "Mikey's not even two. I seriously doubt he's going to get behind on his colors and shapes. I'm talking about us. What are *we* going to do?"

A statuesque brunette swept into the kitchen. "Jennifer! I'm so happy to meet my sister at last—or my almost-sister. I mean my almost-sister-in-law."

After this torrent of words, the woman swooped in on Jennifer and gave her a perfume-scented hug. "I'm Gabriela, but you can call me Gabby."

Jennifer sealed her lips on the obvious comeback to that nickname.

Miguel pushed back another chair. "Gabby, this is Jennifer Lynch. Jen, this is my brother's wife, Gabriela."

Gabby took a seat across from Miguel. "I'm so glad to meet you…and Miguel. Rob thinks the world of his brother."

"Thank you so much for taking us in on such short notice."

"Rob wouldn't have it any other way, and you're welcome to stay as long as you like." Gabby's gaze bounced to Miguel and then back to

Jen's face, a small crease formed between her sculpted eyebrows.

Roberto's wife didn't have a clue why her husband's younger brother, his fiancée and their child had dropped in out of the blue, and from the guarded look on her face, she didn't want to know. Given her husband's line of work, Gabby probably had years of practice avoiding and denying.

"The kids will be in the pool later. I hope that's okay. We'll have a swim instructor in the pool as well as the nanny."

"I'm sure it's all very safe, but I'd be more comfortable if Mikey waited until I was there."

"Of course. I'll let you know when they're heading out, and we'll have lunch by the pool later." Gabby rapped on the kitchen table. "Finish breakfast first. Let me know if you need anything."

"I will, thanks."

Gabby blew them both a kiss as she floated out of the kitchen.

"Whew." Jennifer pushed away her plate and took a sip of orange juice, sour tasting after the sweet syrup and blueberries. "I don't understand how that force of nature is content to live in a fortress in the middle of the desert."

"I don't think they're cooped up here 24/7. They take trips, go on vacations. I believe they have another house somewhere. It's not as if their lives are under constant threat."

"Then I'm glad they were here when we needed them."

She started to gather up the plates and Miguel put a hand on her arm. "I think there's an army of people on staff to take care of mundane things like the dishes."

"I suppose." She continued stacking the dishes. "But it still seems rude to walk away from this mess."

"I'm with you there." Miguel picked up the serving dishes, still brimming with food. "I'm looking forward to playing with Mikey in the pool. Hell, I'm looking forward to playing with Mikey anywhere."

"Well, you're going to have plenty of time to play with him here."

"I'll take those." Miguel took the plates from her and pivoted toward the kitchen.

Gracie materialized again on silent feet. "Leave them, senor. We will take care of all."

"Thank you." Crossing his arms, Miguel wedged his good hip against the kitchen island. "Do you want to take a tour of the house?"

"You mean like of all the bedrooms and bathrooms and the music room and the screening room?" Jennifer rolled her eyes. "I'll take a pass."

"Actually—" he took her arm and pulled her out

of the kitchen "—I mean of the guard tower, the surveillance equipment and the weapons cache."

"Oh." She widened her eyes. "That's more like it. Is Roberto going to show us around?"

"Roberto's busy. His head security guy is going to do the honors. He's meeting us at the foot of the staircase in a few minutes."

"I take it Gabby doesn't exactly know why we're here."

"She doesn't and Roberto doesn't want her to know anything."

"Seems to be a common state of affairs for her."

"It's safer. Roberto is just protecting his wife." Miguel's jaw tightened. "If you hadn't been targeted already, I never would've told you what was happening, never would've involved you in this craziness."

She reached up and cupped his tense jaw with one hand. "I'm not Gabby. I want to know what's going on."

Miguel took her hand and led her to the stairs.

They ran into a burly security guard in dark slacks, crisp white shirt and a holstered gun strapped across his body.

He cleared his throat. "I'm Vin. You folks ready?"

Jennifer squared her shoulders as she faced the big man. "Show us everything, Vin."

And he did. The tour of the house's security

took just over an hour. Miguel asked enough questions to take over Vin's job at the end of the tour.

Roberto had not only instituted the physical security of his compound, but its cyber security, as well—blind IP addresses, anonymous email accounts, a private server—the house had it all. Nothing that came in or out of the house was traceable.

At the end of the tour, Miguel shook Vin's hand. "Impressive. I hope Roberto gives his clients this same tour. They'd trust him with anything if he did."

"He does and they do." Vin glanced at his phone. "Mrs. Eastwood is ready for you at the pool."

"Tell her we'll be right there." Jennifer held out her hand. "Thanks for the tour."

When Vin left them at the staircase, Miguel gestured to his shorts. "I'm ready. Do you have a swimsuit?"

"I did throw one in. You go ahead and keep an eye on Mikey at all times." She tugged on the back of his T-shirt. "How's your hip? You probably shouldn't get those stitches wet."

"I'll be on the sidelines, but I'll watch Mikey." He gave her a chaste peck on the forehead. "Take your time."

When he turned, Jennifer dashed up the stairs. She had no intention of taking her time, not that she didn't trust Miguel to watch Mikey. Pools and toddlers struck fear into her heart, no matter how many lifeguards, nannies or even daddies were out there.

She dug her bikini out of her suitcase and pulled it on, followed by the shorts she'd put on that morning.

She'd seen the pool shimmering in the moonlight last night from the sliding glass doors in the great room and hurried back downstairs.

Stepping outside, she released a pent-up breath when she saw Mikey sitting next to Miguel on the side of the pool, its blue water lapping gently against the sides, devoid of people.

Gabby waved from a chaise longue when she saw Jennifer step onto the patio. "I knew you didn't want Mikey in the pool without you here, so I made the kids wait to get in."

"How thoughtful of you. Thanks."

Gabby's full lips twitched. "Not all that thoughtful. I know how toddlers can get and I didn't want a meltdown on the pool deck."

"Mommy, Mommy. Pool?" Mikey grabbed her around the legs and pointed to the water.

"Of course." Jennifer shimmied out of her shorts. "Where'd you get the swim trunks?"

"Bobby's."

Gabby lifted a lemonade off a passing tray. "I hope you don't mind. He's wearing some of Bobby's old trunks and a swim diaper."

"Thanks." Gabby thought of everything. Her husband might be a fixer, but she was clearly the fixer on the home front.

Holding Mikey's hand, Jennifer walked to the edge of the pool and sloshed down the wide steps into the cool water, leaving Mikey with his toes curled over the lip of the pool, his arms outstretched.

Jennifer turned to face him. "Are you ready?"

Mikey jumped into the pool and Jennifer caught him beneath the water.

Miguel clapped on the sidelines as he settled on the pool's edge, hanging his legs into the water. "Good job, Mikey."

Jennifer dog-paddled across the pool, towing Mikey along and then played retriever while he hung on to Miguel's legs until Miguel kicked his legs out and Mikey let go.

After about the tenth time, Miguel asked, "Will he ever get tired of this?"

"Maybe after another ten times."

Roberto's son Bobby floated past on an air mattress, with the private lifeguard pulling him along.

Mikey pointed and splashed.

The lifeguard stopped. "Can he hop on for a ride?"

"Okay." Jennifer held on to Mikey as he floated to the air mattress on his back. Then she put him on top. "Stay on top. He's taking you to the deep end."

She joined Miguel at the side of the pool, hooking her arms along the edge and kicking her feet in front of her as she watched Mikey playing. "This is nice, but I don't know how long we can stay here."

"As long as we need to."

After playing in the pool for another hour, wiggling his toes in the hot tub and eating lunch, Mikey curled up and fell asleep under the shade of an umbrella.

Gabby waved at Julie, the nanny. "Mikey needs to go inside for his nap, Julie. It's too hot out here for him to be sleeping, even in the shade."

Miguel broke away from his brother, who'd come down to the pool for lunch. "I'll carry him inside."

Jennifer sipped her lemonade and closed her eyes. This parenting gig was a lot easier with a second body to share the load. Now if they could only settle into some normalcy, even if that meant Miguel getting deployed again. That kind of separation she could endure because she'd done it before.

She must've dozed off in the sun. Her eyes flew open when Miguel sat on the edge of her chaise longue. She blinked behind her sunglasses and surveyed the quiet patio. The kids had all packed it up and must've followed Mikey inside for naps.

Roberto looked up from his laptop. "I told Miguel he'd better wake you. This sun is unforgiving, especially reflecting off the water and the pavers."

Jennifer laced her fingers and stretched her arms in front of her. "Impressive fortress you have here, Roberto."

"Impenetrable. You'll be safe here, Jennifer."

"And Mikey, too." Gabby tossed her magazine to the side. "Maybe we'll even take a little getaway with the kids and by the time we return Miguel will be back."

Roberto made a sharp movement, and Miguel shifted his position on the chaise longue.

Wings fluttered in Jennifer's belly. "Be back? Where would Miguel be going?"

"Oh." Gabby swung her long legs off the chaise longue. "I thought... Oops, I have to feed the baby."

The fluttering had reached Jennifer's chest. "Miguel? What did Gabby mean?"

Roberto snapped his laptop shut and pushed back his chair. "This is a discussion for the two of you."

Jennifer watched Roberto duck into the house before turning to Miguel, her jaw tight. "What's this discussion we need to have? Where are you going?"

"Jen, I can't just sit here waiting. I need to find out who infiltrated the agency. I need to clear my name."

"And what am I supposed to do?"

"You're going to stay here—with Mikey. I'm not going to put you in danger—not anymore."

Chapter Eleven

"The hell I am, Miguel Estrada. You're not going to shut me out any more than you already have."

Miguel met Jennifer's blazing blue eyes with an unflinching stare even though her anger sizzled between them, hotter than the desert sun. Why did he think there was ever going to be a good time to tell her she was staying behind?

"That's crazy, Jennifer. I haven't shut you out at all."

The way her cheeks flushed as her eyes flashed fire made his stomach dip. She hadn't missed his reluctance to get physically close to her. Had he really fooled himself that she hadn't noticed? Especially given the way things used to be between them.

She flicked back her damp hair. "Whatever. You can keep your secrets if you like, but you're not leaving me here. I just got you back. I'm not letting you go."

"Think of it as a mission or deployment." He squeezed the back of his neck where his tense muscles bunched.

"I would, and you know I understand your job, but you're Stateside now and I'm with you and just as involved as you are."

"What about Mikey?"

"You and Roberto's head security guy just spent over an hour selling me on the safety of this place. Gabby and her cadre of household help, including the private tutor, nanny and lifeguard, will be able to keep Mikey safe—a lot safer than he would be out there." She flung out one hand toward the high wall that encircled the house and grounds.

"So would you be." Miguel hunched forward, resting his forearms on his knees.

"I can't believe you'd even consider leaving me behind, Miguel. I thought you knew me better than that."

"I know you're stubborn." He locked his fingers together and blew out a breath. "This is different from that other stuff."

"Is it, really? You once broke it off with me because of some misguided belief that you could protect me from your family—the very family we're staying with now, I might add. You almost broke it off with me again when you went overseas for your first deployment." She leaned forward and cinched both of his wrists with her fingers. "When are you going to get it that we're in this together? I'm here for the long haul. I'm not going to run off like your mother did—besides, the circumstances are totally different. Your mom was escaping from the criminal activity of your father, not from the idea of standing beside him."

"My mother…"

"Your mother had good reason to bail, but you're not a criminal like your father. Let me be there." The pressure of her grip increased until her fingers were biting down to the bones of his wrist. "You need me, Miguel. Don't think I haven't noticed."

He yanked his arms from her grasp, his mouth dry. "Noticed what?"

"C'mon, Miguel. You barely sleep. When you do, you have night sweats. I've seen your hands tremble, even though you try to cover it. And you—" she jumped up from the chaise longue "—you're not interested in making love to me."

Miguel closed his eyes against the bright sun. "It's not that I don't want to, Jen."

"I know." She dipped down and dragged one foot in the water. "You were a prisoner of war. Your captors tortured you, did things to you that you don't want to reveal to me, but you have more than physical scars, Miguel. The enemy scarred your psyche, too. You're not ready to be out there on your own. You need my help."

He collapsed in his chaise longue. He'd always wanted to be there for Jennifer, be her protector as his father never was for his mother. Now he felt like a failure—just like his father. "You see me as weak."

Her flip-flops slapped against the pavers as she marched toward him. "You're the strongest man I know, but it's not some fake macho strength you possess. It's the kind of steel that runs bone-deep—the kind that allows you to withstand months of torture without breaking. The kind that demands you escape from comfort and security once you realize there's a price to pay for that security. The kind that launches you into action to protect your son when you've been a father a mere few days." She perched beside him and took his face in her hands. "But you need the strength now to recognize that I can help you."

He swallowed. "What if I can't protect you out there, Jen?"

Dropping her hands from his face, she tipped her head back and laughed. "Because you've done such a bad job of it so far? You rescued Mikey from a burning room. You saved him from a kidnapper. You dragged me away from an exploding car. And you vanquished a villain in a ball pool. I'd say you're batting a thousand, slugger."

He scratched at his beard for a minute. "You'll need a fake ID."

"Now you're making sense." Jennifer sat at his feet, crossing her legs beneath her. "Roberto can handle that, can't he?"

"He's handling it for me, someone he has on retainer."

"Where are we going first?"

Jennifer had been right. He needed someone to have his back if he hoped to root out the mole. Besides his sniper teammates, he couldn't think of anyone he trusted more than Jennifer. He could still protect her even if she came along for the ride.

"We're going back to the debriefing center in Maryland." He placed his whole hand on top of her head. "But you'd better listen to me, follow my lead and do what I tell you when I tell you."

She twisted her head around and saluted. "Of course. I trust you to keep me safe, but you have to trust me to keep you safe. If I see you're pushing yourself or if your health falters, then it's your turn to listen to me."

He saluted back. "It's a deal."

"Has Roberto already contacted someone about an alternate ID for you?"

"She's coming tonight."

"She?"

"Roberto claims she's an artist—ID, fake documents, creates a whole new identity."

"We'd better let Roberto know she'll be creating two."

Later that evening, after a dinner with enough Italian food to feed an army, Jennifer sat on the edge of Mikey's bed while Miguel read his son a story.

Mikey's eyes would drift closed and then pop open if Miguel stopped reading.

"He doesn't want the story to end." Jennifer pulled up Mikey's covers and blinked. "I've never been away from him for more than a few days."

Miguel closed the book and whispered, "I don't want it to end either."

Jen grabbed his arm. "Mikey will be safe here, won't he?"

"You've seen the house and grounds. I can't think of any place he'd be safer. The woman coming tonight is also going to create some fake documents for Mikey, just in case."

"In case of what?" Her grip on his arm tightened.

"In case they have to make a quick getaway with him. Roberto also has a helicopter and a private jet at his disposal." Miguel smoothed his thumb down Mikey's cheek. "In the unlikely event something happens here, Roberto can get away—out of the country, if necessary."

"I'm praying that's not going to be necessary." Jennifer pushed up from the bed and stood next to the window.

"I'm praying for a lot of things right now, Jen."

Miguel came up behind her, wrapping his arms around her waist.

She leaned against him. They kissed. They touched. He was afraid to do more.

Jennifer shivered and Miguel tightened his hold. "Are you actually cold in Palm Springs?"

"It's the AC." She hunched her shoulders. "It's blasting."

A light tap at the bedroom door saved him. He crossed the room and widened the door for Vin. "Yeah?"

"Lena's here. They're in the kitchen."

"Thanks, Vin. We'll be right down."

When the head security man left on silent feet, Miguel joined her at the window again. "Are you ready?"

"Let's do this."

He took her hands. "You don't have to come with me, Jen. I can handle myself."

"But if you leave me again, I won't be able to handle *myself*."

Downstairs at the butcher-block table, Lena unfolded her long, lanky body as she rose to shake their hands. "I know this is a special assignment for Rob, and I'm gonna do my best— untraceable ID's and cards. The credit cards can't even be tracked after you use them."

"I'm going to load up Miguel with enough cash so he doesn't have to use the cards, Lena."

She narrowed her eyes. "You always have to

use cards, Rob, and if he makes any airline reservations and pays cash, that's gonna raise a red flag."

Roberto spread his hands and shrugged. "I'll leave it to the expert."

"Is this your look?" Lena wiggled her long fingers in Miguel's face.

Miguel tugged at his beard. "I've been trying to grow out my beard, and my hair hasn't been this long since high school."

"And what about you, blondie?"

Jennifer raised her eyebrows. "Are you suggesting I change my appearance?"

"Damn right, I am." Lena pointed to a black suitcase parked in the corner. "I have supplies—maybe some brown hair, shorter. You can either cut and dye it, or find a wig."

"What do you suggest?"

"If this were just for one event, I'd go with a wig. But if you're on the run for more than a few days, in and out of hotels, I'd go with the dye job."

Miguel reached over and combed his fingers through the strands of her hair. "As long as you put it back to its natural shade when this is all over."

"When this is all over, I'll shave my head if you like."

Lena put her hands on her hips and faced Roberto. "Rob, I know you don't like involving

Gabby, but damn that woman has a way with hair and makeup."

"She'd be happy to do it." Roberto dragged his phone across the table with one finger and typed in a text.

Lena drove a knuckle into Miguel's chest. "It's best that your hair stays dark because of your coloring, but your hair is more brown than black, so we can take that darker."

"You want me to dye my hair and beard?"

"You wanna fly under the radar as much as you can?"

"Yeah."

"Dye job for you, too." Lena pulled some papers from a briefcase on the table. "While we're getting your appearance sorted out, we can start working on some of these forms."

Gabby bustled into the kitchen on a wave of perfume and a clap of her hands. "Hello, Lena. Where's your stuff?"

"My suitcase is in the corner." Lena flicked the ends of Jennifer's hair. "Darker, shorter and more glam all around."

"Glam?" Jennifer shot a look at Miguel, and he shrugged.

"I'm assuming the people after you know what you look like?" Without waiting for an answer, Lena snapped three times down the length of Jennifer's body. "They know you as the wide-eyed, blue-eyed blonde with the girl-next-door vibe. That's gotta change if you don't want them picking you out in a crowd or spotting you on surveillance tape."

Jennifer nodded as Gabby grabbed her arm.

"I know just what to do, Jen."

About forty-five minutes later, after Miguel had signed some forms and gotten a new birth certificate and Social Security number, his fiancée returned to the kitchen a changed woman.

He tucked Jennifer's chin-length brown hair behind one ear and gazed into a pair of chocolate-brown eyes, heavily made up to look even darker, bigger and more mysterious. "Whoa. You look totally different."

Jennifer spun around. "I don't know how I'm going to re-create this look on my own."

"It'll be easy, Jen." Gabby tucked a makeup kit into Lena's suitcase. "I cut your hair in a blunt cut so that it will practically style itself when you dry it. You already wear a little makeup. Just apply it heavier and use these colors instead of your neutrals."

Lena shoved some papers toward Jennifer. "You can keep whatever makeup Gabby used from my stuff to get that effect. Nobody looking for Jennifer Lynch is going to notice a smoky woman of mystery."

Jennifer batted her eyelashes at Miguel. "Did you hear that? I'm a smoky woman of mystery."

"I only hope I can remember who you are."

"Your turn, Miguel." Gabby crooked her finger. "I have a black color all ready for you."

After Gabby had turned his brown hair and beard black, they returned to the kitchen. Lena then took their pictures for their new identities and assured Roberto that she'd have everything delivered to the house tomorrow.

"This calls for a celebratory drink." Roberto clapped his hands together and broke out the good tequila again, setting up several shot glasses on the table and filling each one to the top.

Miguel snagged a glass, clinked it with Lena's and poured the smooth, pale gold liquid down his throat. "Thanks, Lena."

"Your brother's the boss." Lena bit into lime and downed her own drink.

Roberto poured another round, and after Miguel disposed of that one, he tipped the bottle into his glass for a three-peat. He met Jennifer's eyes across the table, no less stormy in brown than they had been in blue.

She hunched forward and whispered, "Are you still taking those painkillers?"

"Just one." He held up an index finger, which wavered a bit but didn't tremble, and threw back his third shot of tequila, looking forward to the fuzziness around his brain that had allowed him to sleep last night—sleep without waking up once.

Gabby gave Jennifer a quick hug and a peck on the cheek. "I'll leave you all to celebrate. I'm going up to bed."

"Thanks for all your help, Gabby. We have another few days, so I'll try to duplicate this look under your watchful eye."

"You'll do fine." Gabby winked broadly. "Lucky Miguel—it's like he gets to sleep with a different woman without cheating on his woman."

Everyone in the kitchen laughed and Miguel joined in, but Jennifer's face sported two red spots on her cheeks.

She dropped her head, the new hair creating a dark curtain across her face, and reached for a shot glass brimming with tequila. She raised the glass. "Here's to cheating on your woman with your…woman."

Giggling, Gabby left the group with a wave of her hand.

Roberto poured another shot for Lena, but she pushed it away. "I have to get home to my girlfriend or she'll think I've been cheating on her."

Miguel took the drink meant for Lena and dumped it into his own glass. "Thanks again, Lena."

"Good luck, you two. I'll send all the documents over tomorrow."

Vin appeared and helped Lena pack up her

suitcase and equipment after she dropped a makeup bag on the table for Jennifer.

A sudden silence descended on the kitchen and as Miguel reached for the bottle, Roberto snatched it. "I know the doc realized you'd had a few last night when you took that painkiller, but let's not overdo it. I've never seen you overdo it, Miguel."

Miguel closed his eyes and rubbed his temple. "It's the stress."

"I understand, but I think you've had enough to take more than a few edges off." He gave Miguel a one-armed hug. "We'll talk tomorrow, bro."

Roberto hugged Jennifer and whispered in her ear loud enough for Miguel to pick up, "Do you need help getting him upstairs? You can always use the elevator."

"I can walk." Miguel patted his new black beard.

Roberto chuckled. "Okay, okay. Good night."

Good night? Damn right it would be a good night. Any night he could sleep all the way through, blissfully blacked out, was a good night.

Jennifer waited for him by the entrance to the hallway, and he wove toward the dark-haired beauty.

She took his arm. "Do you want to use the elevator?"

"Sure, let's live it up."

She rolled her eyes and guided him toward the elevator tucked next to the staircase. Like magic, it delivered them to the second floor.

Miguel stumbled into the bedroom and fell across the bed. Blackness edged around him, seeping into his mind, obliterating all other thoughts and memories—except one.

The memory of his bright, shiny girl had kept him alive, had allowed him to hang on to the edge of sanity when it had been slipping away from him.

That dream now stroked his chest and whispered in his ear. "Why, Miguel? Why won't you make love to me?"

He groaned and shifted to his side, toward the soft voice that kept him afloat. "I want to, Jen. More than anything, I want to make you mine."

"Then why don't you? I'm right here."

Soft lips caressed his, but the alcohol, the drugs, the pain, the rage prevented him from reacting with a physical response. Thank God.

He mumbled a response instead. "I can't."

"Why, Miguel? Why?"

"Because I'm afraid I'll kill you."

Chapter Twelve

After a restless night, Jennifer woke up with a start, her heart pounding in her chest.

Before she reached for him, Jennifer felt Miguel's body heat signaling his presence beside her this morning. Once he'd uttered his shocking statement last night, he'd passed out, looking anything but dangerous.

She'd tried to stay awake all night, not because she feared he'd make good on his prophecy, but because she wasn't about to let him escape this morning without an explanation.

Sound asleep, his black beard covering his lean jaw, his lids closed over his watchful eyes, Miguel almost looked like a stranger. She trailed her fingers down his arm and traced the outline of his hand splayed on his T-shirt, covering his stomach. She blinked back tears. This man would never be a stranger to her. He'd captured her heart the moment their eyes met down the length of that bar in San Diego, the bar she and her girlfriends had descended on with the express purpose of meeting some hot navy SEALs in training at Coronado.

Her plan had worked out perfectly, except Miguel hadn't been interested in a quick hookup. He'd told her early and often he wanted forever—and he'd gotten it with her.

If he thought he was going to scare her off with his scars—physical or otherwise—he'd picked up the wrong woman in that bar.

He huffed out a breath and rolled to his side, away from her.

She crowded his back, draping an arm around his waist and flattening her hand against his belly.

"Jennifer?" He mumbled her name into the pillow.

Resting her chin on his shoulder, she flicked her tongue at his earlobe. "Have you forgotten already? Do you think you're in bed with some strange brunette?"

He grunted and shifted onto his back again, dragging one hand over his eyes. "I feel groggy."

"That's what happens when you mix booze and pills."

"Ugh." He ran his tongue along his teeth. "I need to brush my teeth."

He made a move, and she grabbed his biceps. "You're not going anywhere, Miguel, until you tell me what you meant last night and why you have to get blotto before you can get to sleep."

"Did I say something stupid last night?" He slid up to a sitting position and bunched up the pillow behind him.

"Don't try that with me." She poked him in the chest. "You know what you said, and I'm sure you meant it. Now I want an explanation—for everything. I-if you can't have sex because you're not physically capable, you can tell me that. I'm not going anywhere, ever."

His eyebrows jumped to the hair tousled over his forehead. "Is that what you think?"

"It crossed my mind. Why wouldn't it? You endured months of torture."

"I still have all of my equipment and it's in working order—as far as I know." He reached for the waistband of his jeans, which he'd never removed the night before. "Do you want to check?"

"Yeah, I wouldn't mind, since I haven't seen your…equipment since you came back from the dead, but you're not going to distract me from my mission here." She punched her own pillow. "If you're physically able to make love to me, why won't you?"

Miguel sucked in his bottom lip and stared at a point off in space. Then he tapped his head. "I can't do it mentally, Jen. I'm afraid of losing control. I'm afraid of what I might do to you."

"That's ridiculous. Even if you're not as psychologically…sound as you were before your captivity, there's no reason to believe losing control, as you put it, is going to result in some violent reaction from you during sex."

Pressing his palms on either side of his head, he squeezed his eyes closed. "You don't get it."

"You're right. I don't get it, so why don't you start explaining it to me."

His eyelids flew open and he pinned her with his dark, intense gaze. "My captors brainwashed me. They elicited violent behavior from me with certain triggers."

His words hollowed out a pit in her stomach, but beneath his probing gaze she kept her face a mask of concern and sympathy. "That's barbaric."

"That's one word for it."

She swallowed her fear. "What about the doctors in Germany or Maryland? Surely, you didn't see just medical doctors. You must've received some psychiatric treatment, too."

"You're kidding, right?" He crossed his arms and hunched his shoulders. "These are the same people who implanted a GPS under my skin. Do you think they were concerned about my mental health? In fact…"

"In fact what?" She held her breath, all of a sudden wanting to chicken out from the truth she'd probed out of him.

"I think the people at the debriefing center

continued the brainwashing. My violent dreams and imaginings didn't stop when I was there. They may have even intensified."

"Is that why you don't try to go to sleep without passing out first? The dreams?" She tried to take his hand, but he wouldn't uncurl his fist clenched beneath his arm.

"It's not just dreams. It's actions while I'm asleep, sleepwalking. Things I've done in my sleep that I can't believe happened."

"Maybe they didn't happen, Miguel."

"What do you mean? They were staged?"

"Or not. Maybe they just told you what you did in your sleep, and it was all lies."

He shook his head. "Some mornings I saw the results of my actions—bloody knuckles, other prisoners beat up and, later, hospital rooms destroyed. And the memories. I had memories of doing these things."

She bent her knees and pulled them up to her chest, wrapping her arms around her legs. "That's the sleeping. What about the lovemaking?"

"It worries me."

"Obviously. Why?"

"It's that loss of control."

She turned her head toward him and rested her cheek on her knees. "Okay, I don't want to deflate your male pride here but while the sex between us is undeniably hot and mind-blowing, it's not like we forget who we are and what we're doing."

Her words coaxed a smile from his lips. "Don't worry. My pride's intact."

"So, that brings me back to square one. I don't understand what you have to fear from making love to your fiancée, even if you don't want to fall asleep in my arms after."

"Jen, the violence they embedded into my brain? It's against you."

She pressed a hand to her galloping heart. She whispered, "Why would they do that?"

"To cause the maximum amount of psychological damage. If they'd known about Mikey—" the veins of Miguel's neck bulged out "—I'm sure they would've included him in the sick fantasies they drilled into me."

"How did your captors even know about me?"

"When they got me, they got my phone. Your picture is all over my phone—and they used it against me. Used you against me."

She shoved a tuft of hair behind Miguel's ear. "Just because you have violent dreams featuring me and have even acted out in your sleep doesn't mean any of that is going to surface for you when we make love. We've kissed, touched, spent time together cooped up in a car, and I've never seen one flick of temper from you—not toward me anyway."

"But it could happen. I don't feel one hundred

percent. The only way I feel safe falling asleep is if I'm facing total obliteration of my consciousness. There's a reason why people turn to alcohol to drown their feelings."

"You're talking to the daughter of a recovering alcoholic. Ask Mom if that works."

"It works for me, especially taken with the painkillers."

"Maybe Roberto knows a psychiatrist. In fact, I'm sure he does since he seems to know everyone else."

"We're leaving tomorrow. I don't think a shrink can help me in one day."

Extending her legs, she rolled to her side, facing Miguel. She hooked one leg over his. "Maybe I can help you dispel some of those demons, or at least put one to rest."

"Maybe." Miguel uncrossed his arms and threaded his fingers through her newly dark hair.

"Mommy!" The door of the bathroom that joined their room to Mikey's burst open and Mikey barreled into the room at high speed.

He stumbled to a stop and fell forward on his knees.

"Silly boy. Are you okay? Come on over here."

Mikey tottered to his feet, his eyes wide. He walked to Miguel's side of the bed and grabbed his father's arm. "Mommy funny."

"Oh." She fluffed the ends of her hair. "I just changed my hair."

"Mommy yellow hair."

"That's what I say, kiddo." Miguel hoisted Mikey onto the bed.

"Now Mommy has brown hair, just like you." Jennifer touched her finger to Mikey's crinkled nose.

His face broke into a wide grin and he clambered across Miguel's body to get to her. She pulled him close and stroked his cheek.

"Mommy and Daddy are going away for a little while. Remember when you stayed with Grandma and Grandpa when Mommy went away?"

"Gamma?"

"This time you'll be staying with your cousins, right here."

"Bobby?"

"Sounds like he already idolizes his older cousin as much as I idolized Roberto." Miguel chucked Mikey beneath his chin. "That's right. You get to stay with your cousins while Mommy and I go on a trip."

Mikey twisted a lock of Jennifer's hair around his fingers as he shoved the thumb of his other hand into his mouth.

Jennifer sighed and rubbed her nose with the back of her hand. "This is not going to be easy."

"You can always stay here with him, Jen. I can manage on my own."

"No, you can't." She leaned close and whispered in his ear. "Mikey will be well guarded here and out of harm's way, while we'll be rushing into God knows what."

Miguel reached around Mikey to clasp the back of Jennifer's neck. "I hope to that same God I'm able to handle whatever comes our way."

Did Miguel still think she was the only one who needed protection?

Entwining her arms around her son, she reached for the man she loved. Just as she'd lay down her life to protect her son, she'd walk through the burning flames of hell to keep Miguel safe and bring him back from this edge of madness where he currently resided.

She'd either have to bring him back or join him.

LATER THAT DAY, their fake ID and documents arrived with Lena's assurances that they could use the credit card, book travel and even buy a car and vote in the state of Oregon.

As she and Miguel sat alone in the great room, Jennifer cupped her new driver's license in her palm and read aloud, "'Karen Tedesco.' Ooh, Lena made me a few years older."

"She gave me glasses." Miguel twirled around a pair of black-framed glasses by the arm.

Jennifer replaced all her documents in the manila folder, but tucked the license into her purse.

"Roberto told me Dr. Paz is coming around to check on his patient. How's the hip?"

"It feels fine. I'm sure the scar will end up being a lot smaller than some of the others."

"I wonder if our stalkers followed that GPS to San Diego." She chewed on the edge of her nail.

"They probably did, although they'll know by now we outfoxed them and that makes me feel pretty damned good."

"When we hit the road again, they'll have no idea where we are—that makes *me* feel good."

"They probably won't guess that I'll be heading back to the lion's den."

"Just how do you plan to sneak back into that lion's den?"

"I'm working on it."

"You don't think it's dangerous flying right into DC?"

"How so?"

"That's not flaunting ourselves right under their noses, right in their backyard?"

"It'll be a good test for our new ID's."

Roberto opened the sliding door to the patio and poked his head into the room. "Everything look okay? Did Lena do a good job?"

"She did a great job, Rob." Miguel pushed up from the sofa and met his brother at the door. "I don't know how to thank you for everything you did—are going to do."

Roberto lifted one shoulder. "I have a lot to

make up to you, Miguel. I followed Dad into the criminal life, leaving you no role models, no kind of family life to hold onto. How you made it into the navy and stayed on the straight and narrow, I have no idea. You're a stronger man than I am."

"Part of my sniper training was a psychological assessment, and I learned a lot about myself. I learned a lot about you, too, and your motivations." Miguel flung out his arm to the side. "You're no Boy Scout, Rob. I suppose a fixer can't be completely clean, but what you do is no dirtier than politics and politicians travel in all the right circles. You've come a long way. You have a great family, and I've come off my high horse."

"Miguel, you stay on that high horse—someone in this family has to." Roberto gripped Miguel's hand in his. "And when you're done with whatever it is you have to do, your son will be waiting for you and you can all pick up the life that was snatched from you in those caves in Afghanistan."

Jennifer bounded up from the sofa and embraced both Estrada brothers. "I'm ready for another group hug."

Vin stepped into the great room with Dr. Paz in his wake. "The doc's here, Miguel."

"Why don't we do this upstairs this time?" Miguel pointed at the ceiling. "Everyone's out at the pool, but they'll probably be coming in soon."

"Lead the way." Dr. Paz patted his black bag.

Jennifer tucked her hand in the crook of Miguel's arm. "I'll come with you. I have a few questions of my own."

She ignored Miguel's sharp glance. "We can even take the elevator."

"I've been in that elevator many times." Dr. Paz rolled his eyes. "And don't ask me what I was doing here or whom I was treating."

When they got to the bedroom she and Miguel were sharing, the doctor checked out Miguel's stitches. "Looks good. They should be dissolving in under a week. Still taking the antibiotics?"

"Yes. I think I have three days left on those."

"You can drop the painkillers if you like and swap them for ibuprofen."

Jennifer held up her finger. "I was going to ask you about those, Dr. Paz. Do you think you can give Miguel another bottle of painkillers, or something else?"

Dr. Paz's gaze bounced between her face and Miguel's. "I thought he wasn't going to take any at all."

A muscle ticked in Miguel's jaw, right above his new beard. "It's not my idea, Doc. I can lay off the painkillers anytime."

"Dr. Paz." Jennifer placed her hand on Miguel's tight shoulder. "I don't know how much of Miguel's history you know, but he was a prisoner of war and he's still suffering from post-traumatic stress disorder."

Miguel's whole frame stiffened. "Jen."

"It's true. He can't sleep. He has bad dreams, so he doesn't want to sleep. He's not in a position right now to get treatment, but he will when that time comes. Can you help him?"

Shrugging her hand from his shoulder, Miguel said, "You need to butt out, Jen."

"I'm sorry, Miguel, but I knew you wouldn't ask him yourself and I don't want to see you suffer anymore. Besides, you need to sleep if you're going to get your strength back."

"Are you done?" Miguel's eyebrows collided over his nose and he vibrated with irritation.

"That explains a lot." Dr. Paz peeled off his gloves and sealed them in a plastic bag. "I can give you a sleeping aid. It's a lot healthier for you at this point than alcohol, and definitely safer than mixing pills and alcohol. It'll put you into a relaxed state and then a deep sleep."

Dr. Paz dug into his bag and pulled out a bottle. "Definitely not something you want to become dependent on, but it's a stopgap until you can get the counseling you need."

"Looks like you're both ganging up on me." Miguel's hand closed around the bottle and he shoved it in his front pocket.

"You're going to thank me for those." Dr. Paz zipped up his bag and tucked it under his arm.

They walked Dr. Paz downstairs and Vin escorted him out to the helicopter pad.

When the thwacking of the blades died down, Miguel rounded on her. "I didn't appreciate that…meddling, Jen."

"You heard Dr. Paz. You're going to thank him—and me—for those pills when nighttime rolls around." She flipped her newly dark hair back from her face. "Besides, you call it meddling, I call it self-preservation."

"So, you *do* think I'm going to attack you in my sleep."

"No, but I'm depending on you to protect me and you need a good night's sleep—every night. How long do you think you can go on sleeping upright in chairs or setting the alarm on your phone to wake you up after an hour's catnap or, worst of all, drinking and drugging yourself into a stupor?"

"You're right." He pinched the bridge of his nose. "The sleeping pills will help with all that, and I do need to be in top form to succeed at this mission."

"I'll take care of you, and you'll take care of me." Curving an arm around his waist, she pressed a kiss against his shoulder. "Now, let's go spend the rest of the day with our son before we have to leave him tomorrow."

LEAVING MIKEY PROVED even harder than she imagined. He clung to her on their last hug, but was still excited to be staying with his cousins.

His mommy's absence would probably hit him in a day or two, but Gabby assured Jennifer that they'd videoconference every day.

When they pulled away from the desert compound in a car they'd borrowed from Roberto, with their phony ID's and a wallet full of cash, Jennifer blew her nose.

Miguel skimmed his knuckles down her thigh. "Are you okay?"

"I'm fine. It's better that we leave him there instead of dragging him out on the road to face who knows what. That truth makes me feel better." She jerked her thumb toward her laptop in the backseat. "That and modern technology. Being able to see each other, even if it's on a computer screen, is going to make the separation a little easier."

"Do you think he's going to forget me?" Miguel's hands tightened on the steering wheel. "We were just getting to know each other."

She stroked his forearm. "You made quite an impression on him. He's not going to forget his daddy. You'll be getting your mug in front of the camera when we video chat to remind him."

"I'm not going to let you hog the camera time—count on it." He took a sip of coffee. "We've got two hours before we get to the airport in LA. You can sleep if you want."

"I don't need it. I slept well last night." She

drummed her fingertips on his arm. "And so did you. No dreams?"

"Not one."

"You haven't heard anything from Josh Elliott yet?"

"I checked our chat room last night. He's on another mission, so he probably doesn't have a lot of free time. I'll give it another shot when we get to the airport."

Staring out the window at the collection of giant wind turbines, Jennifer twisted a strand of hair around her finger. "I hope we don't get stopped getting on the plane."

Two and a half hours later, they sailed through security without so much as setting off a beep with a buckle.

Juggling her laptop and coffee, Jennifer poked through the wrapped sandwiches in a refrigerated container. "What sounds better, turkey and pesto or chicken and sun-dried tomato?"

"They both sound awful." Miguel reached past her and grabbed one of the sandwiches she'd looked at and discarded. "I'm getting the roast beef. Do you want some chips?"

"I'm going to skip the chips. Ever since I had Mikey, I've had to keep tabs on my calorie intake."

Miguel snorted. "You look great to me."

"You haven't really seen me with my clothes off, have you?"

Miguel raised his eyebrows and jerked his head toward the woman perusing the salads.

Hunching her shoulders, Jennifer grinned. Served him right. "Maybe I should get a salad instead."

"Get the turkey pesto and I'll share some of my chips and my cookie with you. It's a long flight."

They found two seats facing the window and settled in for the forty-minute wait before their flight started boarding.

Jennifer tucked her coffee cup beneath her seat and pulled out her laptop. "I'm going to check my emails. I want to make sure my grades were approved."

"I don't have any emails to check, but I'm going to visit that chat room."

She slid a glance at him as she logged in to her computer. "It's not a dating chat room, is it?"

He raised two fingers Boy Scout fashion. "I know nothing about dating chat rooms and wouldn't even know how to access one."

"So, where are you two meeting, or is that classified information?"

"Nothing is classified information as far as you're concerned."

"Not anymore."

"It's a message board for a TV show." He flicked the screen of his laptop.

"That's clever and random. Nobody would be

looking there for messages from you. Do you have code word screen names and everything? Secret decoder rings?"

"I wish." He tapped his keyboard. "I'm Chi Guy—*C, H, I*—because literally I have no connection to Chicago at all. And Josh is Tom58."

"Because…?"

"Because it means nothing."

"Yeah, I think you guys should stick to your day jobs. You could at least have some meaningful screen names."

"I'd love to be sticking to my day job."

She tucked her hair behind her ear and pulled up her email. She deleted the ads and double-clicked on the message from the school that confirmed her grades were accepted for the school year. At least that was one worry off her mind.

Next she double-clicked on a message from Gabby. Smiling, she nudged Miguel's arm. "Gabby sent a picture of Mikey eating his breakfast.

"Miguel?" She turned her head and her heart stuttered when she took in Miguel's taut face and bouncing knee. "What's wrong?"

"Josh sent me a message and it's not good."

"Tell me."

"The word's out—I'm a traitor to my country."

Jennifer put her hand on his. "What does that even mean?"

"It means they're going to use all their resources to bring me in and once they get me there, they have the doctors on their side to label me as crazy or a traitor or whatever it takes so that I'm not believed. The mole must know I'm onto him—and he must be powerful."

"You have people who believe you, Miguel. You have Josh and your other teammates."

"They don't matter now. Josh indicated the rumor is that I turned and set up that SEAL team, that it was me who led them into the trap."

"D-does Josh have any suggestions?"

"He wants me to work with Ariel."

"I thought he had suspicions about her."

"He did, but she handled his situation so well that he's backtracking on that. He thinks she's the only one who's gonna get me out of this."

"What if it's all a setup?"

Miguel dragged his fingers through his hair. "Not Josh, never Josh."

"I don't mean Josh. What if Ariel is whispering sweet nothings into Josh's ear to get him to soften you up? She gained his trust to bring you in."

"I don't know, Jen." He snapped the laptop closed and shoved it into his case. "I've been thinking about how I'm going to draw out this mole. It's going to take some counterintelligence. Just like my original capture when someone planted intel to get us into those mountains, I'm going to have to plant some information that's going to lure out a rodent."

"You're going to have to get proof, Miguel. If this mole is high up in the food chain, nobody's going to believe you without proof."

"I plan to, but it all goes back to that debriefing center." He circled his finger in the air like he was drawing a bull's-eye. "There is something rotten to the core there, and I'm going to find out what it is."

ON THE PLANE, Miguel tried to engage Josh again, but his teammate hadn't responded to his questions yet.

Jennifer poked at the screen in the seat back in front of him. "This one's a good movie."

"I've seen it."

"How'd you manage to see it? It just came out last year."

"In between getting poked and prodded at the debriefing center, I kept busy watching movies, especially at the beginning when I was having headaches and couldn't read or concentrate on anything for long periods of time."

He sucked in his lower lip as he studied the title on the screen.

"Are you remembering something?"

He scratched his beard. "Voices. Those early days I was still pretty drugged up, zoning in front of the TV. The doctors would talk about me as if I weren't in the room, or at least in the next room, and I guess they knew what they were doing because I don't remember what they were saying—only that they were talking about me."

"That's the kind of thing you could recall, Miguel. It's just reaching back to those memories."

"I don't know what I would discover if I could remember. It's not likely they were saying anything important in front of me."

"You never know. They thought you were out of it." Jennifer leaned across his tray table and tapped his screen. "Let's watch it anyway—together."

Miguel flipped up the arm between their seats and pulled Jennifer's hand into his lap. "Anything is better with you, Jen."

He nuzzled her ear. "Have I even told you how much I love you? Maybe this break from everything at thirty-five thousand feet is just what we need. Let's snuggle up and watch the movie."

"Sounds like heaven." She picked up his earbuds and stuffed one in his ear, while she took the other.

As they flew across the country, anonymous Mr. and Mrs. Tedesco watched two movies, ate their sandwiches and even had a couple of beers. By the time they arrived in Washington, DC, Miguel felt like nothing had changed between him and Jennifer—but it had. A boy waited for them in California, and Miguel planned to do whatever it took to get that boy's parents back to him.

They made their way through the airport and collected their suitcases from baggage claim without incident. Their new ID's hadn't flagged anything. Lena was a pro.

The muggy air closed in on Miguel as he stepped outside and dragged their bags toward their rental car.

"Whew, feels like Texas." Jen clasped her hair in a ponytail and fanned the back of her neck. "I guess we missed the nice spring season of cherry blossoms."

"I was here during that season, too, only I didn't see many cherry blossoms."

She stuck her hand in his back pocket. "We're going to have to come back here after...everything."

They navigated through traffic to their hotel, and Lena's fake documents got them checked in without one raised eyebrow.

Miguel stood by the window, looking out onto the busy street. "First I need to secure a weapon and more cash. Roberto is helping me with that, too."

"Have you figured out a plan yet?"

"I have to lure out the mole and the best way to do that is by offering myself as bait."

Jennifer pulled out her laptop and tossed it

onto the bed. "We went through all that trouble—even cutting my hair—so you can let them know you're in DC?"

"It's gonna be a game of cat and mouse, Jen. I have to trip him up, make him show his true colors."

"While you figure that out, I'm going to check in with Gabby." She sat cross-legged on the bed and opened her laptop. "Do you want to say hi to Mikey?"

"Of course." He joined her on the bed while she accessed the videoconferencing app.

Minutes later they were waving at Mikey's smiling face.

Gabby reappeared, eating an apple. "Glad you got there safely. I'll tell Roberto. He had an emergency meeting. He said he gave you some instructions, Miguel."

"I'm all set. Don't worry about us. Just take care of Mikey."

"Like he is one of my own."

Jennifer ended the session and then fell back against a stack of pillows. "He seems fine, doesn't he?"

"He does." He tickled the back of her knee. "Let's go out and get some dinner."

"Do you think it's safe?"

"We're in disguise, and it's not like I'm going to come face-to-face with someone from the center, or the navy for that matter. Even if I do, it'll be a good test."

"Josh indicated you're a wanted man. Do you think that put you on an FBI watch list or something?"

"Maybe if Miguel Estrada or even Raymond Garcia tried to get on a plane or book a hotel room there would be a problem, but Miguel and Ray are not going to do that, are they?"

"I guess I don't know what to expect, and that makes me nervous."

"Then let's have some dinner and talk it over."

Miguel picked a crowded, popular restaurant in Georgetown to put Jennifer at ease, but it had the opposite effect.

She glanced over her shoulder for the third time since they'd taken their seats, and then almost knocked over her water glass as she reached for it.

"It's okay, Jen." He threaded his fingers through hers. "The little men in the white coats are not going to come in here and drag me away."

"Yeah, they might just wait until we've eaten."

"Are you sure you don't want a glass of wine?"

She tapped his glass of iced tea. "I see you're not drinking, probably because you want a clear head. So do I."

"You don't need a clear head. You need a relaxed mind."

"I'd be more relaxed if we'd gone to a little quiet, dark place."

"We can't skulk around in the shadows. We have work to do here." He scanned the room through the clear lenses of his glasses. "Besides, I don't recognize one person here, except a senator over in the corner."

Jennifer snatched her hand back from his and covered her mouth. "You're kidding."

"He's not dangerous—at least not that I've heard."

She spoke through parted fingers. "Will he know about you?"

"I doubt it. I don't believe he's on any defense committees. My so-called defection isn't even going to be on his radar."

"Defection." She crossed her arms and hunched her shoulders. "That sounds so...serious."

"It is serious, if it were the truth."

The waiter delivered their food, and Miguel pointed his fork at Jen's plate. "Eat. I'm expecting a delivery at the hotel from one of Roberto's associates."

"I'm not even going to ask." She peeled back the shell on her crab and stuffed a piece in her mouth.

"You look totally content right now with your mouth full and a little dribble of butter at the corner of your lips." He reached forward and dabbed her mouth with his napkin. "I want to remember you just like this."

"Really?" She took a swallow of water from her glass and pressed her own napkin to her lips. "Believe me, I clean up a lot better than this."

"I know."

Miguel stopped in midchuckle and gripped the end of the table.

Jennifer hunched forward. "What's wrong?"

"You know how I assured you that nobody from the debriefing center would be in this particular restaurant? I underestimated the power of coincidence or fate or just bad luck."

"Who is it? Did he see you?" She kept her head still, her neck stiff.

"She, and she didn't see me, or if she did, she didn't recognize me." Miguel adjusted the glasses on his face just to make sure. "She's a nurse, low-level. Her name's Maggie."

"Even if she's low-level, a way to make herself high-level would be to turn in the traitor. We should leave."

"She didn't notice me."

"How do you know? Maybe she's on her cell phone right now reporting you."

"Nope." He swept a fork through his mashed potatoes. "I can see her from here. She's on a date."

"So, she's not even thinking about you." Jennifer shoved her plate away. "I'm too nervous to eat now."

"We're fine, Jen. You know, I have a feeling even if she did recognize me, she wouldn't be running to tell anyone."

"And you know that, how?"

"Not everyone at the debriefing center was evil. I think one or two people were calling the shots and everyone else was under some false impressions about what I was doing there."

"Do you believe you can actually get some help from somebody there? Is that what you're thinking?"

Miguel took off his glasses and wiped the lenses on the edge of the tablecloth. "It's a thought."

After they both refused coffee and dessert, the waiter dropped off their check.

Miguel pulled some cash out of his wallet and tucked it on the tray. "Now you're going to earn your spot on this team and make contact."

Jennifer's mouth formed an O, which matched her round eyes. "Make contact with...?"

"Maggie."

Chapter Thirteen

"Are you nuts?" She spit out the words between clenched teeth. "The only contact I'd like to make with Maggie is my fist to her nose."

"Fierce." Miguel clamped the money against the tray and held it out to the approaching waiter. "It's all there, thanks."

"You're serious, aren't you?"

"We may need someone on the inside and seeing Maggie here tonight is a sign. She was sympathetic."

"What am I supposed to do? Where will you be?" Jen folded her hands in front of her on the table like one of her own eager students. She wanted more than anything to help Miguel and stuffed down the fear she didn't want him to see. Fierce. That's what she was.

"I'm going to the men's room, and you'll head out of the restaurant. You'll bump her table, apologize and then say you recognize her from somewhere, maybe nursing school because you're a nurse, too."

"I don't know anything about nursing. I don't want to be put on the spot or caught in a lie." She squeezed her hands together even tighter.

Miguel must've noticed the death grip she had on herself because he smoothed the pad of his thumb across the back of her hand.

"You dug a GPS out of me and then did a pretty good job of bandaging me up. She's not going to start quizzing you. Turns out you two didn't go to nursing school together, but you know her from somewhere. Keep it light. Just make contact."

"I can do that." She chewed on her bottom lip. "Do you think Maggie ever saw my picture?"

"Absolutely not. Those files were not part of my medical records." He pushed back from the table. "Are you ready?"

"It's now or never." She wiped her palms on her skirt and waited until Miguel disappeared beyond the bar.

Taking a shaky breath, she stood up and hitched her purse over her shoulder. She held her cell phone in her hand and stared down at it as she passed Maggie's table. She twisted slightly to the right, and her purse hit the side of Maggie's table knocking the empty bread basket to the floor.

"I am so sorry." Jennifer bent over and swept

up the basket from the floor as Maggie and her date assured her that it was empty anyway.

As Jennifer rose and placed the basket on the corner of the table, she widened her eyes. "I know you."

Maggie's dark eyebrows formed a V over her nose. "You do? I'm sorry. I don't recognize you."

That statement gave Jennifer a little more courage, and she snapped her fingers. "I never forget faces. Names on the other hand… Nursing school? Were you in my class at the University of Virginia?"

Maggie's frown deepened. "No. I didn't go to Virginia, but I am a nurse. Maybe we attended some conferences together? Where do you work now?"

"Oh, I'm currently unemployed. You?"

"I—I'm at a government facility." Maggie picked up her fork. "Small world though."

"Isn't it?" Jennifer's smile took in Maggie's date, who nodded impatiently. "I'm sorry about the bread basket and sorry for interrupting your dinner. Have a nice evening."

Jennifer glanced over her shoulder, but either Miguel hadn't made it out of the bathroom yet, or he'd sneaked past her already.

With a slight wobble to her knees, Jennifer walked to the front of the restaurant and staggered outside. She continued a few more steps and then braced her hand against the wall of the brick building, the rough texture against her fingertips bringing her back to a sense of reality.

"How'd it go?"

She jumped at Miguel's words. Then he took her arm and walked her down another block past the restaurant.

"Congratulations. You made contact."

"I got through it and she didn't have me arrested, although her companion looked like he wouldn't have minded. Now what?"

"Nothing yet. It's just a seed planted."

"Did she notice you or look at you when you walked past her table?"

"I didn't give her a chance. I went out through the bar."

She grabbed onto his hand with both of hers. "Now that the panic has subsided, I feel strangely exhilarated."

"You may feel high enough to walk through Georgetown back to our hotel, but it's been a long day and I'm beat."

"And you still have to meet Roberto's guy."

"Roberto's guy is making a delivery to our hotel—top-notch service."

Jennifer babbled in the taxi back to the hotel nonstop—partly riding the adrenaline rush of her interaction with Maggie and partly from the nervousness of being in a hotel room alone with Miguel.

Unlike Miguel, she didn't fear that he'd lose

control and strangle her in the middle of sex, but she did fear his rejection of her. She wanted him now more than ever. They didn't have Mikey with them to interrupt. They didn't have Miguel's family members around and their attendant household staff and security guards.

This situation presented the perfect opportunity for them to reconnect as lovers. She needed the warmth and the strength from his body...and he needed the reassurance that he wasn't some damaged, brainwashed soldier prone to violence.

When they reached their hotel room, Miguel took off his glasses and scratched at his beard for the hundredth time. "I'll be happy to shave this thing off."

Settling her hands on her hips, she tilted her head. "I kinda like the beard and I definitely like the longer hair. I've never been able to run my fingers through your hair before."

"You've never been able to pull it before either, so that's a plus."

"That depends on why I'm pulling it." She fluttered her lashes. "Who knows? You might like it."

Someone tapped on the door and Miguel put a finger to his lips. Placing one hand against the door, he leaned in to peer through the peephole. "It's Roberto's guy."

"Are you sure?"

"Positive." Miguel opened the door and propped

it open with his foot as he accepted the box from the man.

They didn't even exchange one word. Miguel removed his foot and let the door slam on the man's back, as he was already on his way. He placed the box on the table by the window and whipped out the same knife she'd used to gouge his flesh.

She crossed the room and hovered over his shoulder. "Do you know what's in it?"

"I know there's an untraceable gun and bullets in there." He used the blade to slice through the tape across the seams of the box and flipped back the cardboard.

"Ah, this is a little beauty. Leave it to Rob."

Miguel lifted a gun from where it nestled in the box and caressed it like she wished he'd touch her.

"Nothing beautiful about it. Looks like a gun to me."

He glanced up from his admiration of the piece. "Guess it's not your thing. What else is in there?"

She clawed through the shredded paper and pulled out two boxes of bullets. "Bullets for your new friend. And a couple of cell phones."

"In case we have to dump ours." The gun clicked as he began to load it. "Anything else?"

"Oh, my God." Her fingers traced the edges of stacks of bills. "There's a whole bunch of money in here, too. Didn't Roberto give you some cash when we left?"

Miguel plunged his hand into the box and withdrew a bundle of bills. "I got the impression from Roberto that you can never have enough money in his line of work. I guess he figures my line of work right now is no different."

"Now we have something to put in that hotel safe." She plucked stack after stack of cash from the box and lined up each one on the table. "How long does Roberto think we're going to be on the run?"

"It's insurance." Miguel clicked the gun and set it next to the money. "Just like this."

"Now that we have all this so-called insurance, what is our first step tomorrow?"

"I'm going to work on sending some false information out there and see who bites."

"And me?" She patted the cash. "I can try to spend some of this so Roberto isn't disappointed."

"You're going to show up at the center."

"What?" She stopped playing with the money. "How am I going to do that?"

"Not sure yet, but Josh promised me some help on the inside. I'm not alone in this, Jen."

"I know you're not." She wedged her hands on the table, hunched forward and kissed him on the corner of his mouth just visible above his beard. "You have me."

"Let's get this stuff in the safe."

As they emptied the box, they discovered Roberto had also included some pepper spray, mini-cameras, a listening device and a magnetic GPS.

Jennifer dropped the GPS on top of everything else in the safe and swung the door shut. "I've had my fill of GPS trackers."

"That one can attach to a car, so it might come in handy." Miguel's fingers hovered over the safe's keypad. "Combination code?"

"Zero, six, twenty-three."

He punched in the number, and then jerked his head to the side. "The day we met in that bar in Coronado."

A smile curved her lips as she curled her hand around the back of his neck. "You remembered."

"I could never forget that date. It was one of the luckiest days of my life."

"Mine, too."

As they crouched next to each other in front of the closet, facing the safe filled with cash, weapons and burner phones and nothing but danger and uncertainty at their backs, Jennifer knew there was no place else she was supposed to be right now.

She dropped her chin to her chest, touching her forehead to Miguel's. "You're my life, my love."

As he rose to his feet, he wrapped his hands around her waist, bringing her up with him.

When they were both standing he held her close, burying his face in her hair, his beard tickling the side of her face. "*Te amo con todo mi corazón*— with all my heart and my soul, forever."

She slipped her hand beneath his shirt and smoothed her fingers along his back—both the smooth parts and the flesh that had been cruelly tortured. "Show me."

"Jen…" Tension emanated off his body in waves.

She drew back and placed a finger against his lips. "I'm not afraid of you. I don't care what they did to you. You're my man, and I know every cell of your body and every fiber of your being. Since you've been back, you've already shown me over and over again that you're the same man who kissed me goodbye before that last mission. The same man I've been dreaming about for two years. The same man who contributed to a miraculous boy who favors you in every way."

Throughout her speech, Miguel's body had lost some of its tightness. She held her breath as she entangled her fingers in his hair. "Kiss me."

With her urging, he bent his head to hers and brushed her lips with a tentative kiss.

She opened her mouth beneath his, drawing his tongue into her mouth and lightly sucking on it. He deepened the pressure on her lips, and his tongue met hers in a sensuous dance.

Her fingers tightened in his hair, her nails digging into his scalp. She whispered against his lips, "Let's get out of the closet."

He chuckled in her ear, a deep sound that rumbled to her toes. With his hands still cinched around her waist, he walked her backward to the bed until the backs of her knees met the mattress. His fingers scrabbled impatiently at the zipper of her skirt.

She grabbed his wrists. "We're doing this my way."

Splaying his hands in her grasp, he said, "Lead the way."

She dropped her hold on him and unbuttoned the top button of his shirt. She didn't know if she was capable of taking it slow and easy with Miguel, but she had to give it a try. She had to show him that she could set the pace for both of them.

She unbuttoned the rest of his shirt as he stood with his hands at his sides. Then she stood on her tiptoes and peeled it back from his shoulders. It slid to the floor.

She tugged his white T-shirt from the waistband of his jeans, and pinching the edge of it, she drew the T-shirt up his body.

He raised and then crossed his arms, pulling the T-shirt over his head. He dropped it next to his shirt.

She took one step back to drink in his form, still muscular but leaner than she'd remembered.

She stretched out one hand, and trailed her fingers across his chest in a zigzag pattern, ignoring the path of the scars on his skin, ignoring the reason he'd been away from her for two years.

He shivered beneath her touch.

"Do you like that?"

"Mmm." He reached for his fly, but she put her hand over his.

"I'm calling the shots, remember?"

"I remember, but by the time we get around to the main event, I'm going to forget what we were doing."

"I'm not going to ever—" she pressed her lips to a spot right above his pebbled left nipple "—ever let you forget what we're doing here tonight."

He sucked in a breath as her tongue flicked his nipple.

Kissing her neck, he bared his teeth against her flesh. "You know, I'm hard already."

"Doesn't surprise me." She pressed a line of kisses down his biceps. "But what were you telling me recently about the patience of a navy SEAL sniper? You're gonna have to dig deep and practice some of that patience, sailor boy."

She sat on the bed in front of him and skimmed her fingers along the edge of his jeans where they hung on his hips. She twisted open the button on his fly and slid down the zipper.

She peeled open his pants and reached around

to grab his buttocks with both hands, careful to avoid the stitches on his hip. Her fingers dug into the hard muscle beneath the thin material of his briefs.

"I much prefer this to digging a knife into your flesh."

"What a coincidence. So do I." He arched his back, and the bulge of his erection came within inches of her face.

"That's not fair. You're destroying my rhythm here with temptation."

"I'm not a robot. Your hot breath is caressing my package and your fingers are digging into my backside. You can't expect me to stand completely still under that combination."

She choked on her laughter. "My hot breath? Would you prefer my hot mouth?"

"Absolutely." His beard framed his white teeth as his face broke into a smile.

It was the first time that haunted look had left his face when close to intimacy with her. Feeling encouraged, she tugged on his underwear and pulled them, along with his jeans, down his muscled thighs.

Before taking him into her mouth, she scraped her fingernails along the insides of his legs.

"You're a tease." He tousled her hair with one hand. "I think I prefer the blonde who used to do this."

"You just wait. That blonde didn't know

nothin'." She dragged her tongue from base to tip and then sucked him into the depths of her mouth.

He groaned, digging his fingers into her scalp as he rocked against her. His breath came in fast gasps.

She released him, replacing the pressure with her hand and ducking her head to the side and nibbling on his hip.

His body bucked and he growled. "Not fair. When do I get to toy with you?"

"Maybe next time. I'm setting the pace here—nice and slow." And she proved it with the deliberate way she stroked his erection.

Closing his eyes, Miguel threw back his head. "Do I even get to see you naked?"

"If you play your cards right. For now—" she pushed his briefs and jeans down to his ankles "—take these off and stretch out on the bed—on your stomach."

His head snapped up and he opened one eye, pinning her with a dark gaze. "You're kidding."

"Dead serious." She patted the mattress behind her.

Miguel kicked off his pants and brushed past her as he climbed onto the bed. He bent one arm on the pillow and tucked his face in the crook of his elbow.

He sighed. "Do with me what you will."

"I plan to. Just keep your head down." She

pulled her blouse over her head and unzipped her skirt. When she was completely naked she straddled him, placing her hands on his shoulders.

He mumbled into the pillow, his low voice barely audible. "That feels...great."

She squeezed the muscles in his shoulders, digging her thumbs into the back of his neck. "It's so wonderful to touch you again. I've missed this skin-to-skin contact with you. I haven't felt complete without it."

She lowered her body to his, spreading her arms out to her sides, her breasts squishing against the hard, scarred planes of his back. She rested her head next to his on the pillow and whispered, "It's me. It's Jen, the woman you love. The woman you'd never harm in a million years."

He kissed her chin. "I need you."

She sat up again, moving against him, riding him, her knees tucked against either side of his body.

Miguel rolled over, and she fell to the side of him and hooked her leg over his thigh.

"Didn't you like that?"

"I loved every minute of it, but I don't like it when I can't see you. I had to imagine you in my dreams all that time and now that you're here in the flesh, I want to ogle every little part of you. So, climb back up here." He patted his flat stomach.

She straddled him once again, but this time he

reached up and cupped her breasts. "So beautiful, fuller than I remember."

"That's from having a baby."

She clamped her lower lip between her teeth as Miguel dragged his thumbs across her nipples. "Maybe we should have a few more."

He smoothed the back of his hand along her throat, and then traced the sides of her neck to her shoulders with his fingertips as if drawing the outlines of her body. His hands curved with her hips. Then he lifted her up and positioned himself to enter her.

"You've done it, Jen. That edge has melted away and the fear along with it. Can I claim you now as my own?"

"I always was yours, Miguel. That didn't end with your capture. It didn't end with your torture. And it's not going to end as you battle your way back from this nightmare."

Lowering her body onto his, he pushed inside her, and she felt whole for the first time in two years.

He made love to her then, and it wasn't the rough and wild ride she'd come to expect from a night with Miguel Estrada. But at the moment he reached his climax, he stared into her eyes and lit a new flame deep in her soul—one that would never die out.

As he spent himself completely he rolled her

over and rested his head on her shoulder and kissed her collarbone. "You saved me."

"You didn't need saving. You just needed someone to believe in you—and I've always believed in you." She brushed the hair from his forehead. "Doesn't mean we can't have a wild romp now and then, does it?"

"I like a wild romp as much as the next guy, especially with my beautiful fiancée. Am I squishing you?" He slid from her body, beaded with sweat, and draped his arm across her middle. "I'm still going to take one of those sleeping pills Dr. Paz gave me. I don't trust my dreams yet."

"I'll get them since I'm going to grab a bottle of water and make a quick trip to the bathroom. Where are they?" She squiggled from beneath Miguel's heavy arm and planted her feet on the floor.

"In the front pocket of my jeans I discarded on the floor."

Leaning forward, she swept up his jeans and carried them to the mini fridge tucked into the credenza beneath the TV. She retrieved the bottle of pills from his pocket and hung his pants over the back of the chair. As she rose from the fridge, clutching a bottle of water, Miguel's cell phone buzzed and glowed.

"You have a call or a text."

"Can you bring me my phone?"

Jennifer grabbed his phone and returned to the bed. She dropped it next to him, and placed the pills and water on the nightstand.

As she turned toward the bathroom, Miguel swore.

She tripped to a stop and spun around. "What is it?"

"Josh Elliott betrayed me."

Chapter Fourteen

Miguel stared at the text message through a haze of fury. He couldn't even trust his teammates anymore, or did Josh believe the lies about him?

Jennifer was beside him in a matter of seconds. "Impossible. Josh, none of them, would ever betray you."

"Oh?" He curled his hand around his cell phone and read the text message aloud, "'I'm here to help. Ariel.'"

Jennifer blew out a noisy breath. "How is that exactly a betrayal?"

"Josh gave my phone number to Ariel. He must've told her my plan."

"And now Ariel is offering to help. That's a good thing. We need help, Miguel. If you hope to put out some counterintelligence, we need someone on the inside, someone higher up than Maggie."

"This could be a trap. Ariel could be a trap."

"Josh doesn't think so." She rubbed a circle on his chest and he closed his eyes, trying to recapture the sense of pleasure and security Jen had instilled in him.

"You know Josh never would've sent Ariel your number if he didn't have full faith and confidence in Ariel. I mean, even if Josh is mistaken in that faith, and I don't believe he is, he's still on your side. You have a lot of people on your side, Miguel."

He loosened his death grip on the phone. "You're right. I'm overreacting, but I'm not sure Josh is right about Ariel."

"Is there some way you can test her?"

Miguel reached for the bottle of pills and flipped the lid. "I can let her know I want to come in and see who and what she sends."

"Wouldn't you have to take a big risk? If Ariel's not on the right side of things, she could send someone out to kill you and the deed would be done before you even knew what hit you."

"I wouldn't put myself in jeopardy at all if I'm watching from somewhere else." He shook a pill into his hand and popped it into his mouth, followed by a gulp of water.

"How are you going to tell if the person she sends is friend or foe?"

"I'll play it by ear, but I'm gonna need another delivery from Roberto's weapons guy if I hope to pull this off."

Jennifer jerked her thumb over her shoulder at the closet. "You need something more than that little beauty in there?"

Miguel put the bottle of pills and the water back on the nightstand and punched the pillow behind him into submission. He closed his eyes and rested his head against the pillow. "I'm gonna need a sniper rifle."

THE FOLLOWING MORNING, after a dreamless sleep and a dreamy shower with Jen, Miguel put his order in with Roberto's contact. The man promised delivery that night.

Miguel tapped the corner of his phone on the table where he sat, as Jennifer exited the bathroom after drying her hair. "He's delivering the weapon tonight, so I'm going to hold off on contacting Ariel until I have the rifle in my hands. But we can start phase two of this operation."

She looked up from buckling her sandal. "There's a phase two?"

"There is now, and it involves you…and Maggie."

"There is no me and Maggie."

"Not yet there isn't, but you're going to run into her again today."

"That was a pretty big coincidence seeing her last night at that restaurant. I don't think we're going to be struck by lightning twice in two days."

"That—" he rapped his knuckles on the table "—was not a coincidence. That was fate. Today the meeting is going to be by design."

"I can't exactly go to her place of work, can I?"

"No, although I don't think I ever told you the compound where I was treated sits behind a prosthetics and rehabilitation center. Wounded vets can go there to get fitted with their prosthetics and to work out."

"I can't go wandering in there either, can I?"

"No, but it's not far from a shopping center that everyone at the rehab center frequents. They stop by for coffee in the morning, pick up lunch. There's even a bar where some of them get together after work."

Jennifer finished putting on her sandals and stood up, stomping her feet. "Which of these fine establishments am I going to stalk?"

"You're too late for the coffee run and there's no guarantee she's going out for drinks tonight, so that leaves lunch, sandwiches or noodles."

"What am I going to try to get out of her?"

"Anything, everything. Maybe you could say you're looking for a job here." He reached into his pocket and pulled out the listening device. "And you're going to wear this for me, so I can pick up everything you're saying."

"Will you be able to talk to me?" She crossed

the room and pinched the microphone between two fingers, picking it up.

"It's one-way." He reached for the neckline of her blouse and hooked a finger around her bra strap. "You can attach the mic here, and I should be able to hear everything the two of you are saying."

"What if she's not alone?"

"She'll be alone unless the schedule has been changed. Maggie gets a lunch break at one o'clock because she comes in at nine, the same time as Terrence, and she and Terrence hate each other and never have lunch together."

"And if she's meeting a friend?"

"You've already shown yourself to be pushy. You'll join her and her friend." He ran his thumb between her eyebrows to smooth out the frown there. "You wanted to come along. You wanted to help."

"I wanted to be alone with you." She captured his hand and ran her lips across his knuckles. "I wanted to help you love me again."

"Again?" He stood up and hooked one arm around her waist. "I never stopped, but thank you for last night. I'm not saying I'm cured. I'm not saying I'm not still terrified of my violent tendencies and that I might unleash them on you in a moment of passion, but last night was a start. I felt nothing but tenderness for you last night—passion but tempered with gentleness."

"You always had that in you, Miguel. That's not something your captors could've ever brainwashed out of you."

"Maybe that's why they tried so hard. They knew my thoughts and dreams of you were what kept me sane, grounded and civilized—no matter what they put me through." He rested his chin on the top of her head, gritting his teeth, trying to block out the deeds he'd been forced to commit.

"You're here now." She dug her fists into the taut muscles of his back. "And I'm going to waylay Maggie on her lunch break so we can start figuring out who's who in that house of horrors."

"House of horrors. I like that." He kissed the top of her head. "Let's get some breakfast and check in on Mikey. Do you think he's up yet?"

"He might be, but the rest of the household probably isn't. Let's give Gabby some time to wake up and give her a call around eleven our time, before we head out to my lunch with Maggie."

They ate breakfast at a restaurant across the street from the hotel and went back to the room to videoconference with Mikey.

Miguel got a lump in his throat when his son called him Daddy. Would he ever get over that wonder? Would he ever make it back to Mikey? Even if Miguel didn't, he'd make damned sure Jennifer did.

Jennifer logged off the chat and wiped a tear

from her cheek with the back of her hand. "He doesn't seem to miss me too much, so I didn't want to start the waterworks in front of him."

"He probably forgets about how much he misses you when he's looking at you on a computer screen."

"Oh, I don't mind." She closed her laptop. "I'm relieved that he's happy when he talks to me. If he were sad and crying, I'd lose it for sure."

"He's probably still feeling the excitement of a new place and new kids, but what do I know? You know our son better than I do."

She tugged on the edge of his beard. "Don't sell yourself short. You're a natural with kids, and you took to fatherhood like you'd been doing it for years."

"I hope to be doing it for years to come." He grabbed her hand and kissed her fingertips. "You have a lunch date. Do you have the mic?"

Jennifer patted her purse. "I put it in a little side pocket. When should I put it on?"

"I'll do it for you in the car before I drop you off."

"You sure she'll be at the sandwich shop or the noodle place?"

"In the over four months I was there, Maggie never went anyplace else, especially since the coworker she hated always went to the burger place."

"Don't you love these creatures of habit?"

"Makes spying on them a little easier."

"Is that what we're doing?"

"Let's call it reconnaissance."

It took him forty-five minutes to drive to the shopping center and, despite himself, Miguel felt his palms sweating as he got closer and closer to the place where he'd been held captive a second time.

"Maggie always walks over." Resting a palm on the top of the steering wheel, he pointed a finger out the windshield. "See those coffee-colored buildings in the distance? That's the debriefing center."

Jennifer scooted forward in her seat and dragged her sunglasses down her nose. "What did you say it was on the outside, a prosthetics place?"

"That's what it really is in the front. Doctors really do design and fit prosthetics there. It's partially funded by the Veterans Administration, so there are a lot of vets who go there to get fitted for new appendages."

"Well, at least they're doing something admirable."

"I'm sure the front part of that building doesn't know what goes on in the back part."

He swung their rental car into the parking lot of the mini-mall.

Jennifer pulled her purse into her lap and unzipped it. "I'm ready when you are."

Miguel parked the car behind a large truck on the other side of the parking lot from the restaurants.

Jennifer dropped the mic into his cupped hand. It had a clip on it and he brushed her hair aside and flicked back the collar of her blouse. "I really am going to attach it to your bra strap. Just don't knock it off."

"I don't usually tug at my bra straps in public. It'll be fine there. Do I need to speak up or lean into Maggie when she speaks?"

"No, they're surprisingly sensitive for their size." His fingers brushed the soft skin of her chest as he attached the device to her strap. "Just speak in a normal tone of voice. You're not trying to get anything out of her. Just establish some rapport."

"And you'll be listening to everything we say."

He picked up the corresponding listening device he'd dropped into the cupholder. "It'll all come right through here, and I can record it and listen to it later if I miss anything."

"Hopefully Maggie won't call the police on me for stalking her." She pulled the door handle of the car. "Wish me luck."

Miguel watched his newly dark-haired fiancée march through the parking lot with confidence. His instinct to give her something to do had been right. Even if he didn't expect much out of this meeting, Jen needed to feel useful.

He narrowed his eyes behind his sunglasses. Not that she hadn't been a huge help to him last night. She'd known exactly what he'd needed to ease him into intimacy. And he owed it to her to give her a fully recovered, healthy man and father for their child.

JENNIFER SAT DOWN at the table outside the coffeehouse and pulled out her phone. She kept one eye on the pictures of Mikey Gabby had sent her and one eye on the row of restaurants across the small courtyard.

Ten minutes after Jennifer sat down, Maggie crossed the north end of the parking lot and ducked into the noodle place.

Jennifer dropped her chin and murmured into the mic inside her shirt. "It's noodles today."

Their listening setup was one-way, muted on Miguel's end since he didn't want any noises all of a sudden coming from her blouse. That would be awkward.

Jennifer blew out a breath, jumped to her feet and dumped her half-full coffee cup in the trash. She strode toward the restaurant, amid the thinning lunch crowd, and pushed open the glass door.

Maggie, next in line, didn't even turn around, which suited Jennifer. Let Maggie be the one to discover her.

Jennifer picked up a plastic menu by the front

door and studied it as she shuffled toward the counter where Maggie was ordering. Miguel did tell her that Maggie always ate out, but what if she decided this time to bring her food back to the office?

When she finished paying for her food, Maggie turned from the counter and nearly bumped into Jennifer.

"I'm sorry." Maggie's brown eyes grew round. "You were in Nick's Grille last night."

Jennifer lowered the menu. "Oh, wow. This time *you* almost ran into *me*."

"Couple of klutzes. What brings you out here?"

"The noodles." Jennifer raised the menu. "Someone recommended them."

"Really?"

"Miss, are you ready to order?"

Jennifer turned the menu toward Maggie. "Any recommendations?"

"Number nine."

"Thanks." Jennifer turned to the counter and ordered the number nine and a medium soda. As she filled her cup at the machine, Jennifer watched Maggie take a seat by the window. She snapped a lid on her cup and grabbed a straw.

She started walking past Maggie's table and then stopped. "Would you mind if I joined you? The friend I'm visiting is working today and told me to entertain myself, but I'm kind of bored."

"You're entertaining yourself in DC by eating noodles in a dumpy shop in Maryland?" She tipped her head at the chair across from her. "Have a seat. I'm Maggie Procter, by the way."

"Thanks. Karen Tedesco. I'm kind of burned out on monuments and memorials to tell you the truth."

They chitchatted about sightseeing until they had individually picked up their bowls of noodles and sat back down.

Jennifer clicked her chopsticks together. "I might be looking to relocate in this area. Can you tell me a little more about your job? It sounds more interesting than seeing patients all day."

"Oh, i-it's not really. I help out with the prosthetics team."

"Sounds rewarding. Are they hiring? The government, I mean?"

"I don't think so, but if you want to send my boss a résumé, I have a card." Maggie dabbed her mouth with a napkin and reached into her purse, hanging on the back of her chair. She snapped a card on the table between them and then scribbled on the back of the card. "My boss's name is Emily Stroka."

With the end of her chopstick, Jennifer dragged the card next to her bowl. "Thanks."

Her gaze darted to the red lanyard peeking out of Maggie's purse, sporting the name of the prosthetics company in white letters.

She needed that badge.

As Jennifer reached for her drink, she jerked her hand and knocked over Maggie's cup, sending soda and ice across the table. Jennifer jumped up. "I really am a klutz. I'm so sorry."

Jennifer grabbed the napkins at the table and swirled them around in the liquid pooling on the surface. "Can you get some more napkins?"

Maggie had scooted back from the table to avoid the drips from the edge. "Of course. Maybe they'll get me a towel from behind the counter."

As soon as Maggie turned her back on the mess, Jennifer yanked the lanyard out of Maggie's purse and shoved it into her own.

Maggie returned with two towels and they both mopped up the soda. Righting her cup, Maggie asked, "Can you get me more soda?"

"Of course, but then I'd better get going." She picked up Maggie's empty cup. "What was it?"

"Root beer, heavy on the ice."

"You got it." Jennifer filled up Maggie's cup and returned to the table. "Thanks for sharing your table with me, even though I destroyed it, and thanks for the info. I'm going to head back to my friend's place and wait for her." Jennifer slid her purse from the back of her chair.

"Enjoy the rest of your trip." Maggie was texting on her phone before Jennifer even hit the door.

As she walked at a fast clip across the parking

lot, she spoke into the mic. "Did you catch any of that? I took Maggie's badge. I have a way into that building, and I'm gonna take it."

Immediately her phone rang and she answered Miguel's call as she headed toward the buildings behind the mini-mall. "I'm on my way."

"Stop, Jen. I don't want you going in there."

Her heart thumped harder as she walked faster. "It's the perfect opportunity for me to get in there and snoop around a little."

"You don't even know what to look for."

"No, but I can take pictures with my phone and show you later."

"Do you think they're actually going to have kill orders lying around or stuffed in file cabinets? There's nothing you can accomplish there, Jen, except putting yourself in danger."

"I need to be there. I need to see it for myself."

"I'm still on the outer edge of the parking lot. Come back to the car, and we can maybe plot out a way for you to get an interview with Maggie's boss, although her name doesn't ring a bell with me."

"It's too late, Miguel. I'm going in." She turned toward the gated complex and ended the call on Miguel's sputtered objection. She spoke to him through the mic instead. "I'm sorry. I just have to do this."

Jennifer straightened her shoulders and widened her stride as she approached the gate to the complex. A guard shack stood sentry over the cars driving into the gated parking lot, but nobody manned the revolving door with the card reader.

Jennifer scooped in a deep breath and flashed Maggie's badge at the reader. The red light turned green, the gate clicked and Jennifer pushed through.

"I'm in." She whispered to the fuming listener on the other side of the mic.

The front parking lot catered to the customers of the prosthetics business, with rows of handicapped slots in front of the building.

Licking her dry lips, Jennifer opened the glass door just as a man in a wheelchair was exiting. She held it wide-open for him and he rolled through, thanking her.

She stepped into the showroom and gazed at the lifelike appendages that would bring new hope to their recipients.

A man in a white coat glanced over his shoulder at her. "I'll be right with you."

Then he returned to his conversation with a woman and a man leaning on a pair of crutches.

Jennifer's eyes darted to the side door that led to a quad. She wandered to the display next to the door and slipped through it.

Shoving her sunglasses to the top of her head, she squinted into the window of a building on the other side of the quad. A row of treadmills faced the window and boasted a few walkers and a runner.

That must be the physical rehabilitation center. To the left of that building, there was another, behind a rotating gate just like the one that guarded the parking lot. Unless there was an additional keypad on that gate, Maggie's badge should work for that, too.

No wonder Miguel was able to escape from this facility. The security wasn't that tight, but then it probably hadn't been designed to lock people inside.

She spoke to Miguel inside her blouse. "I'm still alive. I just passed the rehab building and I'm heading for the secure area in the back—the area where they kept you."

She tried not to imagine the steam coming out of Miguel's ears about now. One condition he'd put on her for accompanying him on this mission was that she listen to him and follow his orders.

She'd failed.

She pressed the badge against the reader and sighed when she heard the answering click. She stepped through this gate with a little more caution and strolled to the door facing her.

She twisted the handle slowly and pulled at the door. An empty hallway and computer keyboards clicking from open offices greeted her.

Tiptoeing past the first two offices, she kept her eye on a larger door at the end of the long hallway. The double doors looked like the entrance to a suite of hospital rooms.

A lash of hot anger whipped through her body. After Miguel's ordeal in captivity, his government should've welcomed him home as a hero and given him the best of care, not hidden him in this sterile environment away from his family—away from her and Mikey—where he could've healed so much faster...and better.

"Excuse me."

Jennifer's blood ran cold in her veins. *Don't run.* She tripped to a stop but didn't turn around to confront the owner of the voice. "Yes?"

"Who are you and where are you going?"

Jennifer pasted her best condescending schoolteacher smile on her face and spun around. "I'm here to see Ms. Stroka."

The woman dropped the reading glasses she'd had pinched between two fingers, and they fell against her chest, dangling on the gold chain around her neck. She tipped her head slightly to the left in a jerky fashion. "Who?"

Jennifer poked around in her purse, pushing aside Maggie's badge, which she had no intention of showing to this woman. She pulled out the business card Maggie had given her and read the back. "Emily Stroka. I'd like to apply for a nursing position."

The woman raised her delicate eyebrows a

fraction. She seemed to do everything in small, measured movements.

"How did you get in here? Past the security gates?"

"I piggybacked." Jennifer shrugged her shoulders. "Someone was coming in and I slipped through behind him."

"That's highly irregular and against policy." The woman backed up into her office and leaned across her desk to pick up the phone.

Jennifer's jaw dropped. "Y-you're not going to call security, are you? I just wanted to meet Ms. Stroka in person to chat. You know, make a good impression so my résumé makes it out of the pile."

"That's not how it works here." The woman's nose twitched, but she didn't follow through with the phone call. "This is a government position and you need to go through the jobs website."

"I just thought I could add a personal touch." Jennifer smiled, stepped into the room and plopped her purse down on the desk.

"This person, Ms. Stroka, is not even physically located here. Now, if you don't leave, I *will* call security to escort you out."

"Oh, that's not necessary." Jennifer waved the card once before tucking it back into her purse. "Now that I know Ms. Stroka isn't here, it kinda defeats my purpose. I can go out the way I came in."

"Absolutely not. We can't have unescorted people wandering around our facility." The woman turned and swept a key chain from her desk and hooked it to her lanyard. "I'll see you out."

She gestured toward the door, and Jennifer scooted through it into the hallway. The woman locked the door behind her and waited until Jennifer started walking back toward the offices in the front of the building.

Jennifer cranked her head over her shoulder and peered at the woman's badge. "You're Angela Woodruff? Can I mention on my application that I met you?"

The woman narrowed her cold eyes as she opened the door. "That wouldn't be a very good idea."

Instead of going through the prosthetics showroom, Angela ushered her along the side of the building and into the front parking lot. "I'll watch you from here."

"No problem. I'm leaving."

Jennifer took two steps and Angela stopped her. "By the way, with whom did you piggyback?"

"Some man in a white coat." Jennifer flicked her fingers in the air and marched toward the security gate, feeling Angela's eyes boring a hole in the back of her skull.

She pushed through the revolving gate and

loped across the outer parking lot toward the back of the mini-mall. As soon as she turned the corner of the first building out of sight of the prosthetics compound, Miguel rolled up beside her and she hopped into the passenger seat.

Closing her eyes she tipped back her head. "Whew."

"You completely went off the rails. What happened? The mic even went out. I couldn't hear anything that was going on after Angela caught you in the hallway. Are you crazy? I thought they'd captured you or something."

"Are you done?"

"No, but you are. I can't believe you went rogue on me."

She opened one eye and patted his corded forearm, where his veins stood out from his flesh. "The reason you couldn't hear anything from the mic is because I left it there."

He slammed on the brakes. "Left it where?"

"Right in Angela's office."

Chapter Fifteen

Miguel eased his foot off the brake and the car rolled forward. "Damn."

"My sentiments exactly."

He picked up the silent receiver in the cupholder and gave it a quick glance. "Where'd you leave it?"

"I slipped it onto her desk, near the phone. When she escorted me out of the building, she locked her door. You didn't hear anything?"

"I told you. I thought you'd been found out and the microphone compromised."

"I'm sorry." She rubbed her knuckles along the top of his thigh. "I didn't mean to worry you. It was a split-second thing. I knew I wasn't going to get anywhere near those swinging double doors, so I took my next best option."

"Angela hasn't been back to her office yet, or the microphone is broken."

"I don't think so. I didn't throw it on her desk.

I plucked it off my strap, wiped it with a tissue to get rid of our prints and when she had her back to me I placed it very gently on her desk."

"She could find it, although she does have a messy desk."

"I noticed."

"Problem is, we can't get too far away from her office. The transmitter won't work back at the hotel—too far."

A scratchy noise came over the receiver and Miguel pulled over to the side of the road. He held his breath when he heard the sound of a door close.

Jennifer whispered, "She's back."

Miguel picked up the receiver to clear it from the cupholder and placed it on the dashboard.

Jennifer hunched forward to stare at it.

Angela sighed and clicked on her keyboard.

Miguel said, "Might not be exciting, but at least the sound is coming through."

After a few more minutes of clicking, the phone jangled in Angela's office and both Miguel and Jennifer started back from the receiver.

Angela's stern voice carried through the car. "Hello, Gus."

Jennifer glanced at him and he shrugged. "Never heard of him."

Angela continued after a brief pause, "Good. Did the footage show who let her in?"

Jennifer tensed beside him.

"She badged through? You're kidding. You can track that badge, can't you?"

Jennifer reached over and grabbed his arm, and he said, "Of course they were going to figure that out, Jen."

"I just hope Maggie doesn't get in trouble. I hope they believe that her badge was stolen."

Miguel put a finger to his lips as Angela started talking again.

"Let me know as soon as you find out anything. If we have an employee letting strangers into the facility, we have a problem."

Angela paused again and then shouted into the phone, "That's not your concern, Gus. Just do your job."

When Angela slammed down the receiver of the phone, Jennifer turned a pair of wide eyes toward him. "Wow, she was agitated."

"She runs that part of the facility, so it's on her if it's compromised."

Angela was back on her computer and Jennifer slumped in her seat. "Too bad she doesn't talk to herself."

"This audio setup has a time limit. We can't sit out here all day."

"It's almost two thirty. Will it last the rest of Angela's workday?"

"It's good for four hours, so it'll die sometime between four thirty and five."

She shoved back her seat and wedged her bare

feet against the dashboard. "It's a good thing we had a big breakfast, although I could use some water."

He shook his empty plastic water bottle at her. "Easy for you to say. In addition to that big breakfast, you also had a bowl of noodles and a soda. I heard it all."

"Well, if I weren't afraid to go back to the mini-mall, I'd get us a couple of drinks."

Over an hour later, Miguel shifted in his seat and massaged the back of his neck. "That could be all the excitement for the day."

Jennifer yawned. "I suppose this is what it's like on a stakeout…or sitting on a rooftop watching someone through a sniper scope."

A knock on Angela's door had Jennifer dropping her feet from the dashboard and Miguel clutching the steering wheel with nowhere to go.

"Come in."

"Gus in Security said you wanted to speak to me."

Jennifer clawed at his thigh. "That's Maggie."

"Did he say why?"

Maggie cleared her throat. "Somebody stole my badge and used it to access the facility. Gus said you caught her."

Jennifer sucked in a breath and crossed her arms over her stomach.

"I did. Brunette, hair about this long, medium height, brown eyes. How'd she get your badge?"

"I—I don't know. It was a woman?"

Jennifer's mouth dropped open, and Miguel raised his eyebrows at her and said, "What the hell?"

"You didn't see her?" Angela's tight, low voice had a more menacing edge than her shout.

"No. The last time I had my badge was when I went to lunch at the sandwich place in the mall. I thought I dropped it on the way over or back until I went to report it at the security desk and Gus told me someone had used it to enter the building. In fact, maybe I did drop it and someone just picked it up."

"No."

"No?"

Miguel found himself willing Maggie to keep her voice steady. "C'mon, Maggie."

"The woman who *stole* your badge was waving some card around and asking about a job. I told her she had to go through the dot-gov website for employment. She didn't just randomly find a badge. She knew what she was doing here. I just wish I did."

"Did she explain to you how she got in?"

"She lied and said she piggybacked. So, did you notice a woman around your table or behind you in line?"

"Not really, but I admit to being careless with my badge and just stuffing it in my purse. Maybe this person knows our lunch spots and was waiting for an opportunity. I can't tell you any more."

"All right. Has Gus shown you the video we captured of her entry?"

"No."

"Go back to Security and have a look, and in the meantime, be vigilant."

"Of course, although…"

"Although what?"

"It just doesn't seem like we were so hyperaware until…that one patient."

The silence in the room and in the car seemed to last forever until Miguel had to break the tension. "Uh-oh, Maggie."

"Have you been talking about that patient to anyone, Maggie?"

"Of course not."

Jennifer snorted. "I like the indignant tone. Quite an actress."

"Yeah, but why is she lying about running into you and where she had lunch?" He'd had a good feeling about Maggie, and she'd proved him right.

Angela said, "Good because we might be getting more high-level patients like that here, and we need to practice the utmost discretion."

"I know that."

"Go talk to Gus and keep your badge more secure."

"I will."

The door snapped behind Maggie, and Miguel eased out a breath. "I wonder if that's going to be it. At least nobody recognized you."

"You're sure Angela saw my picture?"

Miguel lifted a shoulder. "She had access to my file because that's where I found it—in her office."

"Wait." Jennifer held up her hand. "Angela's making another call."

"Gail, it's Angela Woodruff. We had an…incident today."

"Do you know a Gail?" Jennifer whispered again as if Angela could hear her.

Miguel shook his head as he listened to Angela tell Gail about the mysterious woman who'd stolen a badge and was wandering around the facility.

When Angela was in listening mode, Miguel said, "Gail is obviously above Angela in the food chain. Angela has an obsequious tone with Gail that she sure didn't have with Gus or Maggie."

Then Angela said something that made Miguel's heart stutter. "You think this has something to do with our missing patient?"

He spoke through clenched teeth. "God, I wish I could hear the other side of this conversation."

Angela listened for what seemed like a long time and then replied. "I will. I will. I will."

Jennifer rolled her eyes. "Very accommodating all of a sudden."

Angela ended the call, or probably Gail ended the call, and the only other word they heard out of Angela was an expletive.

Fifteen minutes later, the reception died. "Not very illuminating except for the name Gail, which I hadn't heard before. I wonder if Angela's going to have the guts to tell Gail about the mic when she finds it."

"*If* she finds it. She might just end up sweeping it onto the floor and Gail would be none the wiser."

"I suppose it doesn't much matter if Gail knows about the mic. She knows the facility was compromised, but the mic isn't going to tell them anything new. It's a cheap device that can be ordered online. Any electronics store would carry it." Miguel pulled away from the curb. "Now I have a name to give to Ariel."

Jennifer whipped her head around. "You've decided to work with her?"

"I don't think I have a choice. I have to trust Josh. We could try to contact Maggie again now that we suspect she's on our side, but she may have been lying to cover her backside. Even if she is covering for you, I'm not going to put her in danger."

"If Josh vouched for Ariel, he must be confident that she can be trusted. She's your best bet." Jennifer tucked one leg beneath her. "When are you going to respond to her?"

"As soon as we get back to the hotel."

Miguel made that happen sooner rather than later, spurred on by a desire to make contact with Ariel...and the grumbling of his stomach.

When they got to the room, Miguel replied to Ariel's message, mentioning the name Gail. She responded quickly with the words, On it.

Jennifer looked up from watching the TV. "Nothing?"

"She's on it, whatever that means." He stretched out on the bed beside her. "Can we discuss dinner?"

"I'm not that hungry."

He poked her arm. "That's because you had lunch while I was stuck in the car."

A phone buzzed and Miguel patted his pocket. "Not mine."

Jennifer twisted toward her phone charging on the nightstand. "It's mine, but I don't recognize that number. Who would possibly have this number?"

Miguel leaned over her. "It's a local DC number. Put it on speaker and answer it."

Jennifer grabbed the phone off the charger. "Hello?"

"Karen, this is Maggie Procter. You know, from lunch today."

Jennifer turned a wild gaze on him and he nodded. Had they just gotten lucky?

"M-Maggie? How'd you get my number?"

"While you so cleverly lifted my badge out of my purse, I cleverly called my number from your cell phone when you went to fill up my drink."

Jen pressed a hand over her heart. "Your badge? I didn't take your badge."

"You can stop with the pretense, Karen, if that's even your real name. I know you took my badge and then used it to gain entry to my place of work. I just don't know why."

"But you made sure to get my phone number using a sneaky method before you even knew your badge was gone? That doesn't make sense."

"What doesn't make sense is running into a woman in a DC restaurant and then seeing that same woman in a Maryland noodle shop—a woman very interested in my job. That's why I got your number."

"I'm not sure what you think you know about me."

"I don't know much, but I have my suspicions and I'm letting you know that I'm on your side if those suspicions are correct."

As the long pause stretched, Jen seemed at a loss for words, so Miguel prodded her hip.

She took a deep breath and managed a squeak. "You are?"

"I'm on *his* side, and I can help."

"How?"

"Meet me for a cocktail. We can talk." Maggie coughed. "If he's with you, bring him along."

Miguel pinched Jennifer's waist and shook his head. He didn't want to confirm his presence here to anyone.

"I'm alone. Where do you want to meet?"

"Where are you staying?"

He didn't even have to lay a finger on Jen this time as she promptly responded. "I can meet you anywhere."

"There's a bar in Georgetown, not far from Nick's Grille. It's called The Insider."

"I'll find it. What time?"

"Seven. I'll be sitting at the bar, and I'll save you the seat next to mine."

"Okay, I…"

But Maggie had ended the call.

Jennifer fell back against her stack of pillows. "What was that all about? How did she make me? I thought I was being so sly."

"Maybe she's paranoid. Maybe she doesn't believe in coincidences."

"Maybe I screwed up. She got my phone. How did I miss that?"

"Don't be so hard on yourself." He ran a hand along her arm. "You were probably so focused on getting her badge, you didn't notice. And she was so focused on getting to your phone, she didn't notice you'd pinched her badge."

"You're not going to let me do this alone, are you? You're going to find some way of being there."

"Of course." He ran a hand through his long hair. "Maggie hasn't seen me since the day I escaped. My hair's longer, darker, I have a beard, I'm wearing glasses and I'm going to become a fan of the Nationals."

"Baseball cap?"

"The gift store downstairs has a bunch of them. I can slouch a little and pretend I'm with a group of people, so I won't stand out. I know that bar. It's a popular sports bar and will be crowded at seven."

"Even if she does recognize you, she is on our side. She proved that today with Angela."

"We'll see. I don't want you to admit to anything at first. Let her talk. See what she has planned out." He tapped his phone in his pocket. "I'll have something new to tell Ariel when she gets back to me, and maybe we can work with Maggie. If Ariel's involved, she can offer more protection for Maggie than I can."

Jennifer scooted off the bed and plucked at the material of her pants. "I'm going to change into something more suitable for cocktails at a Georgetown hot spot. The downside to all this?"

"Yeah?"

"You're gonna have to wait even longer to get something to eat."

"If it means ending this nightmare and getting my family back, I'll gladly starve." He wrapped an arm around her waist and pulled her back down to the bed. "Be careful. If anything seems weird, get out. I'll be nearby, but don't look for me."

Putting her hands on either side of his face, she kissed him—and that was all the sustenance he needed.

JENNIFER SLID OUT of the taxi and smoothed her slim black skirt over her thighs. She puffed out a few breaths and entered the noisy bar. A Nationals game happened to be on several TVs around the bar and she grinned, thinking about Miguel's new cap pulled low over his face. He'd fit right in.

Her gaze swept along the bar and she raised one hand when she spotted Maggie sitting sideways on a barstool, one long leg crossed over the other.

Maggie wiggled her fingers in response to Jennifer's wave.

Jennifer's lips twisted. *Great way for a couple of spies to communicate.*

On her way to the bar, Jennifer squeezed between the tall cocktail tables scattered about the room amid cheering Nationals fans. When she reached Maggie, the other woman raised a martini glass filled with a light pink liquid.

"Since it's just about impossible to get the bartenders' attention in here, I took the liberty of ordering you a cosmopolitan—the best in DC, but then you're not really a tourist or planning to relocate, are you?"

Jennifer sat down and straightened her skirt. "What's your game?"

"Game?" Maggie clinked her glass against Jennifer's, still sitting on the cocktail napkin in front of her, making the pink liquid shimmer in the neon lights above the bar. "It's not a game. It's life and death—Miguel Estrada's."

Jennifer grasped the stem of the glass and sipped the martini, cognizant, as always, of the way alcohol soothed her jangled nerves. "What do you know about Miguel Estrada?"

"I know he's an innocent victim of some very bad people."

"Who are these bad people?"

Maggie responded with a delicate lift of her brows. "I don't have a clue. I only know something wasn't right when he was there, supposedly recovering from his ordeal. The doctors were getting some strange orders, we all were, but we weren't allowed to question them. Security was also heightened while he was there, but the facility wasn't quite prepared for him, or at least his determination, because he escaped anyway."

Jennifer didn't dare turn around to look at the room, but she did raise her eyes to the mirror above the bar, reflecting more than a few men with baseball caps. The caps gave her a warm, fuzzy feeling—better than booze.

Jennifer cupped her glass with one hand and took a long swallow of her cosmopolitan. "What are you proposing?"

"Does that mean you are with Miguel Estrada? Working with him?"

To buy time, Jennifer took another sip of the intoxicating cocktail and then another. She licked the sweet Cointreau from her lips. "What is it you're proposing?"

"I can access some computer files that might explain what's going on, that might clear Miguel's name because he's in a lot of trouble right now. Based on the recommendation of the facility, Miguel's been branded a traitor to his country."

"Why would you do that? You could be putting yourself in—" Jennifer blinked and ran a fingertip around the rim of her glass, searching for the right word "—comfort."

That wasn't what she meant. She shook her head, and the drink she'd just consumed too quickly seemed to slosh in her skull.

"You've heard of whistle-blowers, right?" Maggie tapped the second martini glass the bartender had set down behind the first. "Maybe I want to be a whistle-blower. Hell, maybe I just want the adventure."

"Whistle tune." Jennifer gripped the edge of

the bar, to steady herself in the suddenly tilting room. She ran her tongue along her dry teeth and rubbed her eyes. "I—I think I need some water."

"Try this."

Maggie placed a glass in her hand, and Jennifer gulped back—the second cosmo.

She choked and pressed a napkin to her mouth. "No, no. Water."

Jennifer tried to put the glass back on the bar, but the bar was undulating. When she released the martini glass it dropped and tipped over, spilling the rest of the potent concoction.

A man's voice from far away murmured, "Is she okay?"

Maggie giggled. "We just had a few too many cosmos. I'll get her home."

Home? Her home was with Miguel. With Mikey. How had she gotten so drunk so fast? She tried to form words in protest as Maggie tucked a strong arm around her waist and helped her slide from the barstool.

Jennifer arched her back and tried to twist away from the vise around her midsection.

And then Maggie put her lips so close to Jennifer's ear, and her hot breath stirred her hair. "If you try anything now, if Estrada is here and comes to your rescue, he'll reveal himself—and he'll be a dead man."

Chapter Sixteen

Miguel clapped his new best friend and fellow Nats fan on the shoulder, his gaze darting toward the bar where Jennifer and Maggie had their heads together in deep discussion.

Maggie put an arm around Jen's waist, and Miguel's eyebrows collided over his nose. They'd sure gotten friendly fast. He wished he'd had another mic to send in with Jennifer for this meeting.

Jen's head bobbed, and then she slid from the barstool under Maggie's guidance.

Miguel narrowed his eyes behind the useless glasses and a muscle in his jaw jumped. He cranked his head from left to right, as a cheer went up in the bar at the third strike.

As Maggie led Jennifer away from the bar, one girlfriend helping another who'd had too many fruity cocktails, her bright gaze swept the crowd. Only they weren't friends.

Maggie was on the lookout for him. *They* were on the lookout for him. He'd be damned if he'd let that female viper take Jen out of this bar, most likely drugged, but if he revealed himself they'd both be in trouble.

A chorus of boos went up at a bad call and bodies pressed against his to get a better look at the big-screen TV.

Maggie and Jen had reached the edge of the crowd of sports fans and would have to weave through them to get to the front door. They'd get there over his dead body.

Miguel curled his hand around the gun in his pocket and crouched, so that his head ducked below the shoulders of the man in front of him. He had to get off a shot in this crowded bar without hitting anyone but creating a panic.

Tipping back his head, he took in the Tiffany lamps lining the hallway to the restrooms—the currently empty hallway. He lifted the gun quickly and squeezed the trigger, shattering the glass of the lamp on the end of the row.

People screamed and a press of bodies surged against him. The wave carried him closer to Maggie and Jennifer.

With the weapon still gripped in his hand, close to his thigh, he moved in on them. When he was a foot away, Maggie turned a pair of wide eyes on him. Before she could get off a sound or a signal, Miguel grabbed the back of her neck and squeezed her carotid arteries, cutting off the blood flow to her brain. The traitorous nurse slipped to the floor, releasing her hold on Jennifer.

Several more screams pierced the air as bystanders assumed Maggie had been hit by a bullet.

Lacking the support of her abductor, Jen swayed and listed to her left.

Miguel pocketed his gun and wrapped his arms around Jennifer from behind, propelling her out of the bar like a rag doll amid the chaos, hoping the stampeding patrons were shielding them from Maggie's accomplices.

When they hit the sidewalk, Miguel half dragged, half carried Jennifer several feet along the block. He ducked into a dark restaurant, almost bowling over the hostess at the door.

"What's going on out there?"

"Some shots fired at The Insider."

The hostess pressed her hands against her stomach. "Is she hurt?"

"She fainted. We were almost trampled."

"Oh, my God. Sit down. Has someone called the police?"

As soon as her words ended, a siren screamed down the street.

Miguel edged into the dining room, half-full of people unaware of the chaos several doors down, and settled Jen into a booth, collapsing on the seat beside her. He rubbed her clammy arms. "Are you okay, Jen? Answer me."

A waitress hurried over to their table. "Melody said you came over from The Insider."

"Yeah, shots fired. My wife got crushed in the stampede to get out of there."

"Should she see a paramedic? I just peeked outside and there are several ambulances in the street."

"I think she wants to be as far away from the bar as possible. We don't know if the gunman is done yet." He brushed his hand across Jen's forehead. "Can you bring us some water? Like a pitcher and two glasses?"

"Of course." She scurried off and returned a minute later with a pitcher filled to the brim with ice water and two empty glasses in her other hand. "Here you go."

Miguel filled both glasses with water. "Drink this, Jen, all the way down. If it's some drug, maybe we can dilute it with the water. She didn't want to knock you out completely and have to carry you out of that bar."

He forced her to drink the two glasses of water and then pressed two more on her. In the low light of the restaurant, he detected a decidedly green cast to her face.

"Are you gonna be sick? Can you vomit? That would be the best thing you could do right now."

She nodded, covering her mouth with one hand.

He scooted out of the booth, dragging her along with him and flagged down the passing waitress. "Ladies' room?"

"On the other side of the front door."

They got to the bathroom just in time, and luckily it was a two-stall operation. He crouched beside Jennifer, smoothing the hair back from her damp forehead, as she puked her guts out and then some.

Pale and shivering, she sat back on her heels. "Ugh."

His face broke into a wide smile. "What a beautiful word, your first since I grabbed you from Maggie. Do you think you're done? The more the merrier to get all that poison out of your system."

"Poison?" she gasped and heaved again.

"Figure of speech, probably a drug, a powerful sedative."

She wiped the back of her hand across her runny nose, and he ripped off a length of toilet paper and dabbed it against her upper lip. She took it from him and blew her nose. Then she yanked off a few more sheets and wiped beneath her eyes.

"Feeling more yourself?"

"Yes."

Her teeth chattered and he scooped her up off the floor, her sexy black skirt now a crumpled mess. He held her arm and led her to the sink.

As Jennifer rinsed out her mouth and splashed her face, an older woman pushed through the door.

"Oh!"

"I'm sorry, ma'am. My wife is ill and I didn't want to leave her."

"Bless you, boy. You must be newlyweds." Her eyes twinkled. "Take all the time you need."

Jennifer lifted her head from the sink. "I'm done. I'm okay."

They edged out of the bathroom, Miguel's arm firmly around Jennifer's trembling shoulders. He guided her back to the booth.

"We're staying here?"

"Just until I can call up a car on my app to get us back to the hotel." He dragged his phone from his pocket and accepted their location and selected the nearest car.

"Can I get you something else?" The waitress jerked her thumb over her shoulder. "I heard the police haven't found the shooter yet, but nobody was injured." She took a quick glance at Jennifer. "A-at least no fatalities, but a few people in shock, like you and a few minor injuries from the mass exodus."

Miguel said a silent prayer for the innocent bystanders injured as a result his rescue of Jennifer. He hadn't had a choice. "Thank God for that. We're just going to wait inside for a car, if that's okay."

"Of course. I'm surprised there aren't more stragglers from the bar seeking shelter in here."

When the waitress left, Miguel grabbed Jennifer's hand. "Now what did Maggie say to you before she started to cart you away?"

Dragging her hands over her face, Jennifer puffed out a breath between her fingers. "She said she was on your side. She wanted to be a whistle-blower and expose the people who were setting you up—everything I expected her to say when I thought she was a friend and not a foe. She played me."

"Played us. She was so sympathetic when I was at the center, obviously planted to gain my confidence, maybe even planted to spy on Angela since she kept the theft of her badge a secret from her. She did that to help herself, not you since she had no way of knowing we were listening to her and Angela."

"And *she* had to be the one we ran into at the restaurant last night."

"I think it was fortuitous." He held up a finger as Jennifer started to interrupt him. "We're drawing them out. I now have another name connected to that center to give Ariel."

"She hasn't gotten back to you yet?"

"Not since that brief message earlier." He squared his phone on the table.

"Now the people out to kill you know you're

here in DC." She stirred the ice in her water glass. "I'm sorry I ever stole Maggie's badge."

"Don't be. They would've found out soon enough if Ariel plans to use me to lure them out." The driver called, and Miguel directed him to pick them up in the alley behind the restaurant.

Several minutes later in the backseat of the car, Miguel's phone buzzed and he pounced on it.

"Ariel?" Jennifer asked.

"Roberto's man. He has my…package." Miguel glanced at the rearview mirror, but the driver had his eyes on the road in front of him.

When they got to their hotel room, Jennifer retreated to the bathroom and hunched over the sink. "Oh, my God. I look horrible. Why didn't you tell me I had raccoon eyes?"

He came up behind her and rested his hands on her hips. "I thought they looked kind of cute."

"Is the guy Roberto sent coming to the hotel again like last time?"

"No."

Jennifer raised her black-rimmed eyes to meet his in the mirror. "Why not?"

He shrugged. "Now that we've been outed in DC, I don't want any paths leading to our door."

"Makes sense." She bit her bottom lip. "Where are you meeting him?"

"On the Mall near the Capitol Building, public

place." He ruffled her dark hair. "You're staying here."

"You're leaving now?"

"You'll be okay. I don't have to tell you to lock and latch the door and don't open it for anyone—room service, housekeeping…police."

"Police?" She spun around in his arms until they were chest-to-chest. "Are you going to be okay?"

He pulled her so close their bodies merged. Maybe there was no separation between them? He kissed the top of her head. "I'll be fine. I know this guy. You saw how it went down last time—a quick exchange and on our separate ways."

Miguel waited until Jennifer had washed her face, brushed her teeth and crawled into bed with a bottle of water beside her and her computer in her lap. Then he sat on the edge of the bed and captured one of her nervous hands in his. "Give my love to Mikey. I'll be back soon, but you're going to have to leave your little nest here to lock and latch the door behind me."

She threw back the covers and cupped the side of his face with one hand. "I love you, Miguel."

"And I love you, *mi amor*." He caressed the soft lobe of her ear. Then they walked to the door together, and he kissed her willing mouth. "Now go talk to our son."

He stood outside the door, listening to the clicks that locked his love safely inside. Then he walked to the street and took a taxi to the Mall, still teeming with tourists in the sultry night.

He ambled toward the meeting place, his hands in the pockets of his shorts, his shoulders hunched forward and the baseball cap shielding his face. In case the man couldn't recognize him, Miguel had mentioned the cap. Miguel would be able to spot his contact by the case in his hand.

A couple of men who'd had too much to drink stopped in front of him, arguing about the baseball game, and Miguel sidestepped them. He focused on the man with the case twenty feet in front of him.

"You don't know what you're talking about, buddy." To his right, one drunk shoved the other and charged forward, pulling his baseball cap down over his forehead.

When Miguel saw his contact raise the arm with the case toward the oncoming drunk in the Nationals baseball cap, he swore under his breath and quickened his pace to overtake the man.

Two seconds later, the man dropped, a pool of blood seeping from the back of his head.

Miguel dived to the ground, knocking his own cap off his head. He flattened his body against the pavement and yelled to anyone who would listen, "Get down!"

His contact, Roberto's man, fell to his knees, still extending the case with the sniper rifle tucked inside. His body jerked with a second shot to the head, and he keeled over.

Panic rippled through the pedestrians on the Mall. A woman stomped on Miguel's arm as he reached forward to drag the case toward him.

With people surging all around him, some crouched in defensive positions, some flat on the ground, Miguel crawled forward, pushing the case ahead of him. When he reached the thickest clump of people, he staggered to his feet and loped out of the Mall.

The DC Metro Police were crawling over the scene, warning people to stay down or take cover. Miguel couldn't afford to be stopped by them—not clutching a case with a sniper rifle. Still crouched over, he ran down the street along with others escaping from the mall.

Several blocks away, panting, sweat running into his beard, Miguel forced his way into the backseat of a taxi before it pulled away from the curb. He shouted the name of the hotel.

The taxi driver twisted around. "You coming from that craziness in the Mall?"

"Yeah." Miguel slumped in the seat, closing his eyes.

"What happened back there?"

"Active shooter."

"Damn. There were shots fired in a George-town bar tonight, too. I wonder if this is connected."

"Probably." Miguel couldn't manage another word as dread thrummed through his veins. He had to get back to Jennifer.

The driver dumped him off in front of the hotel, and Miguel made his way to the room, the rifle case banging against his leg. He knocked on the door and Jennifer opened it immediately, dragging him into the room.

"Oh, my God. What happened out there? A special bulletin interrupted the show I was watching." Her gaze flicked to the case at his side. "That wasn't you, was it? The reporter said at least one, possibly three fatalities."

Miguel let the handle of the case slide from his fingers as the case hit the carpet at his feet. "It was me…us. Jen, I'm worried."

"Why?" She grabbed his shoulders. "Are you hurt? Were you shot?"

"My contact mistook another man in a base-ball cap for me. Whoever had him in his sights took the bait and killed the man in the cap, also believing he was me. Then he shot Roberto's man."

"That's horrible." She clutched her hands in front of her. "But you're okay and you got the rifle."

He encircled her wrists with his fingers. "Don't you see, Jen? They ID'd Roberto's man, followed him to get to me, which means they also have a line on my brother. If they know all about Roberto…"

The color drained from her face. "They know where Mikey is—and they may have already gotten to him."

Chapter Seventeen

"What do you mean?" The room tilted, and Miguel's fingers cinched tighter around her wrists to make it stop.

"I—I tried calling Gabby earlier. I can't reach anyone at the house on any of the phones."

Miguel scrambled for his phone and started calling anyone and everyone at Roberto's compound—nothing, dead silence. Clutching his useless phone in his fist, he paced the hotel room. "We need to head back to California—tonight."

"What good will that do?" Jennifer hugged herself around the waist, almost doubling over. "I-if they took Mikey, if they harmed your brother's family, it's all over now."

The phone buzzed in his hand, and Miguel whipped it in front of his face. "It's Ariel."

"It's not about Mikey, is it?"

"No." He swept his finger across the display to reveal the entire message and read it aloud,

"'We have a plan to out the mole. Call.' She gave me a different phone number."

"Call her."

"I don't give a damn about the mole now. I just want Mikey back."

"So do I, but I also want the person responsible for taking him."

"Of course, you're right and maybe if we nail the mole, we can make some sort of trade for Mikey—if they have him. We don't even know that yet." Miguel ran a hand through his hair, his chest expanding with the first full breath he'd taken since those shots were fired.

"We don't. We don't know that."

"I'll put her on speaker." Miguel tapped in the number Ariel had sent him, a tightness forming around his heart.

A low female voice answered. "What happened at the Mall?"

"How did you know that was me?"

"What happened?"

"I went there to meet a weapons supplier. He was made and shot, along with an innocent bystander mistaken for me."

"Did you get the sniper rifle?"

"How did you...? I got it."

"Good, you're going to need it. We've been suspecting a mole for months now on the Vlad task force. This is our chance to lure him...or her out."

"Wait." Miguel wiped a hand across his mouth. "The weapons supplier worked for my brother. My son is with my brother, and I'm worried his identity and location have been compromised."

"We'll check on him."

"His name is…"

"Rob Eastwood. A fixer. Lives in a guarded compound in Palm Springs. We'll check on him."

Miguel's gaze collided with Jennifer's. "What's the plan?"

"A small group of us has been working for over a year to get a direct line to Vlad, although he won't suspect the intel is coming from the US intelligence community. I just used it for the first time."

"Did he bite?"

"We'll soon see. I put out the information that you're meeting with a reporter tomorrow to tell your story. Nobody in the intelligence community has this information. I fed it through the channel to reach Vlad only, and he won't know it came from us. If someone shows up to kill you, we'll know for sure that person is connected to Vlad. I'm also monitoring all communications of the people on the Vlad task force. This person is not going to slip through my net."

"Where's this meeting taking place?"

"Stone Hill Park, near the band shell."

"Plan?"

"The reporter doesn't know you, has never

seen you before. You're showing up with a blue backpack on your back, and the reporter is going to be carrying a red purse. I suggest you show up with the backpack. I'll be standing by with a red purse if I'm needed. I have one person I can trust completely and I'm sending him to the park to wait. Someone approaches you, shove your sunglasses to the top of your head as a signal, and my guy will take the shot."

"So, in case I get killed in the exchange, your guy can still capture the shooter."

"*Our* guy, Estrada, and I don't expect you to get killed. You've survived more than any man ought to."

"I'm not gonna survive if they have my son."

"We have agents in California who are heading to Palm Springs now. Hang tight."

Jennifer sighed and fell across the bed.

Miguel gave her a thumbs-up. "So, I'm going to show up at this park at…?"

"Noon."

"Noon and do what? Just be a target?"

"That's up to you to figure out. I can't spare any more people for this, despite its importance. The only ones who know about the meeting are you, me, the man I'm sending…and Vlad and whoever he tells. That's it. That's the way it has to be."

"I'm supposed to expose myself to a killer?"

"You *are* a killer, Estrada."

Ariel gave him directions to the park and band shell and ended the call.

Miguel swore and tossed his phone onto the bed, next to Jen.

She jumped up from the mattress and walked to the window. "Doesn't sound like much of a plan."

"I think Ariel hopes to nab the mole through the communications she's monitoring. Vlad is going to have to pass this intel along to his person at the task force, and Ariel will pick that up."

"What if you just don't show up at all? Ariel will still have the proof that Vlad contacted someone about the meeting."

"But if there is no meeting, there's no proof. I have to go through with this. I'll walk through the park with my blue backpack and just hope I don't get shot. If nobody takes the bait, the mysterious Ariel will most likely come out of the trees with her red purse, putting herself at risk, too."

"Maybe that's the best way. She should go out there with her red purse to draw out the contact. He's not going to kill the reporter, and then he can be taken out and you won't have to put yourself in any danger at all."

"She's not gonna do that."

Jennifer flattened her hands against the window. "None of this matters anyway if they have Mikey."

Miguel came up behind her and wrapped his arms around her as tightly as he could. "If they had him, they probably would've already contacted me to make some exchange—my life for his, which I'd gladly give."

She leaned back into him, her hands pressing against his thighs. "I'd gladly give my life for both of you."

He kissed her temple. "Let's get to bed. This could all be over tomorrow."

When they lay side by side, she held out one of his sleeping pills and a glass of water. "For the bad dreams."

But before he drifted off, they made love. He hadn't planned on it. He still didn't trust himself completely. Even Ariel had called him a killer. But when he held Jennifer and she sobbed lightly against his chest, worry for their son breaking them both, he took her, and they joined together in their fear and anxiety—and they became one.

JENNIFER SMACKED TWO twenties down on the counter for the red handbag on sale, her resolve stronger than ever.

She wasn't about to let Miguel walk into that park and expose himself to a killer. She'd left him a note in the hotel room this morning that explained how she couldn't watch him walk out the door, asking him to call her when it was over.

Then she turned off her phone and went shopping for a red purse.

At eleven thirty, she made her way to Stone Hill Park. Slinging her new red bag over her shoulder, she strode along the trail until she saw the band shell in the distance.

On this warm summer day, people flocked to the park—joggers, hikers, picnickers—no music lovers. The band shell was empty. Knots of people strolled past her, and Jennifer hugged the purse tighter to her body. Could she draw out this person?

She wandered back and forth in front of the stage, taking deep breaths of the nutty smell of the beech trees towering nearby. If Miguel saw her now, he wouldn't risk blowing her cover and getting them both killed. Hopefully, he wouldn't approach her at all.

She trailed her hand along the bushes, knocking off the little red berries. Then something shuffled behind her.

Swallowing, she turned slowly and met the bright gaze of a man with a blue backpack on his back. He cocked his head.

"Are you Miguel?" Her heart hammered in her chest and she briefly wondered if he could see the furious fluttering of the ruffle on her blouse.

"You're the reporter?"

She held up the red purse, dangling from her fingers. "Yes."

"Good." He took her arm with one hand and pulled a gun out of his pocket with the other. "Now we'll wait for Miguel together. I'm sure he's not going to want to be responsible for your death."

"My death? Who are you? What do you want?"

The signal. The signal. What was the distress signal?

Jennifer stumbled away from the man and shoved her sunglasses to the top of her head.

The man dropped beside her, blood oozing from his head.

Jennifer stood frozen, her feet rooted to the ground. She couldn't just stand here. The man might have an accomplice, a backup.

She lurched forward, zeroing in on the trail ahead of her, winding through the trees. Staggering on wobbling legs, she careened down the path, burrowing deeper and deeper into the shelter of the cool forest until she collapsed against a tree, hugging it, slowly coming to her senses as the bark scratched her cheek.

"Jen!"

She spun around and flung herself against Miguel's solid chest. "Oh, my God, you're okay."

"*I'm* okay. I almost called off the whole thing when I woke up this morning and discovered you missing. I can't believe you put yourself in this kind of danger."

She grabbed his T-shirt with both hands, tears streaming down her face and dripping off her chin. "Without Mikey, I don't think I can go on. Without both of you, I'd die."

"That's not ever going to happen." He cupped her face with both hands. "Mikey's okay. He's safe, and so am I. It's over."

Epilogue

His wife peeked under the towel at their son, sleeping on a chaise longue beneath an umbrella.

The others, Rob and his family and their entourage, had gone inside to the give the newlyweds a little alone time after their whirlwind wedding in Vegas.

Jennifer stretched out beside him on the pool deck, resting her chin on her folded hands. "So, you never saw Ariel or her backup guy at the park?"

"Never. I still don't know who she is or what she looks like. Once I told her my suspicions about what you were up to and that I wanted to be the one on the other end of that sniper rifle protecting you, she gave me carte blanche to do what I wanted."

"And you did." She rubbed his shoulder and then kissed it. "She's satisfied she nabbed Vlad's mole?"

"No question about it. When the counterintelligence was leaked, Vlad set the wheels in motion. The spy Ariel identified made three untraceable phone calls the night before, two more the next morning and called in sick to work. When it became clear that the man at the park was going to use you, the reporter, to get me to come along with him, that's all Ariel needed to see."

"I just wish Rob could've gotten word to us sooner that Mikey was safe. I might not have pulled that crazy stunt, as you called it."

"He didn't want to chance it. Once he knew his man had been ID'd, he figured it was only a matter of time before Vlad's people would pay him a not-so-friendly visit. He knew he had to get Mikey out of here."

"So, this mole, this Jeremy Kartcher, had been feeding Vlad information from the task force all along."

"Yeah, and he's the one who gave the orders to Gail, who then disseminated them to the rest of the rehab center regarding my so-called treatment, and Gail's been removed so the center can get back to what it does best."

"And Maggie?"

"Maggie thought she was following Gail's orders. She didn't understand the ramifications."

"At least it didn't turn out to be your own government trying to kill you."

"I guess that's one silver lining. The other?" He twisted her blond hair around his finger. "I got you to feel sorry enough for me to marry me in a quickie ceremony. I couldn't have waited for what your parents had planned for our wedding."

After a long kiss, she pulled away from him. "Are you going to miss being a sniper?"

"You know my assignment in San Diego is temporary, right?" He tipped his sunglasses to the edge of his nose. "I will be up for deployment again once I'm cleared—physically and mentally."

"I know that."

"Do you have a problem with it?" He held his breath. He'd do almost anything to make Jen happy—almost anything.

She plucked his sunglasses from his face and stroked his clean-shaven jaw with the back of her hand. "I married a navy SEAL sniper and I couldn't be prouder of you."

Rolling on top of her, he straddled her body and kissed every inch of her face. He slipped his hand beneath her bikini top and caressed her soft, warm breast. "And I married a blonde little miss sunshine who turned into a fearless warrior princess. Can I ravage you upstairs, warrior princess?"

"Pool, Daddy."

As Miguel glanced up at Mikey sitting on

the edge of the chaise longue, rubbing his eyes, Jen laughed.

"Welcome to fatherhood, stud."

Miguel did a push-up on either side of Jen's body and swept up Mikey under one arm. "I was made for this."

* * * * *

Look for the last two books in Carol Ericson's
RED, WHITE AND BUILT *miniseries*
in early 2018.
And don't miss the previous books
in the miniseries:

LOCKED, LOADED AND SEALED
ALPHA BRAVO SEAL
BULLSEYE: SEAL

You'll find them wherever
Harlequin Intrigue books are sold!